# ZATHURA

# ZATHURA™

## THE MOVIE JUNIOR NOVEL

Adapted by

ELLEN WEISS

Screenplay by

DAVID KOEPP AND JOHN KAMPS

Based on the book by

CHRIS VAN ALLSBURG

Produced by Intervisual Books, Inc.
Houghton Mifflin Company, Boston 2005

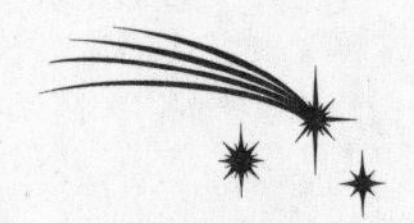

 Published in the United States
by Houghton Mifflin Company, Boston.

www.zathura.net
www.houghtonmifflinbooks.com

Produced by Intervisual Books, Inc.
Houghton Mifflin Company, Boston 2005

QUM 10 9 8 7 6 5 4 3 2 1

COLUMBIA PICTURES PRESENTS A RADAR PICTURES/TEITLER FILM/MICHAEL DE LUCA PRODUCTION A FILM BY JON FAVREAU "ZATHURA"
JOSH HUTCHERSON JONAH BOBO DAX SHEPARD KRISTEN STEWART AND TIM ROBBINS MUSIC BY JOHN DEBNEY EXECUTIVE PRODUCERS TED FIELD LOUIS D'ESPOSITO
BASED ON THE BOOK BY CHRIS VAN ALLSBURG SCREENPLAY BY DAVID KOEPP & JOHN KAMPS PRODUCED BY WILLIAM TEITLER SCOTT KROOPF MICHAEL DE LUCA DIRECTED BY JON FAVREAU

Zathura.com

COLUMBIA PICTURES

TABLE OF
CONTENTS

*THWACK. THWACK. THWACK. THWACK.*

Danny Budwing sat cross-legged on the cool grass, looking to his left, then his right, then his left, then his right—back and forth, back and forth, like someone at a tennis match. He was watching his dad play catch with his big brother, Walter.

With each *thwack* of ball into mitt, the ball hit the pocket a little more loudly. "Nice catch!" "Great throw!" Walter and Dad called out to each other. "Way to go!" They were in exceedingly high spirits.

Dad and Walter knew baseball, that was for sure. They had strong throwing arms. They were good with the glove. They didn't drop any balls.

Danny sighed and rested his chin on one hand.

"Okay, Danny, you're up!" Dad said.

Danny took a deep breath and picked up his glove.

"I didn't get my whole turn!" Walter protested.

"Yeah, I counted," Dad said. "That was twenty-five. That's what we said."

"That's not fair!" Walter howled.

Dad was unmoved. "It's exactly fair. Come on, Danny, time for your turn, and then I gotta work for an hour."

"It's my turn, Walter," Danny told his brother. "Dad said."

Walter shrugged. "Whatever."

Danny scowled as his sweaty, athletic big brother stalked past him, shooting him a dirty look. "You're not the only one who gets a turn, you know," Danny said to Walter's back.

Dad squared off to throw to Danny, moving in much closer than he'd been to Walter. "Okay, Dan. Eye on the ball. You got it this time." He was excruciatingly encouraging. It would have been easier if he'd just told Danny he wasn't any good. It was so hard to be a puny six-year-old when your brother was nine and good at everything.

Danny jammed the glove onto his hand, hit the pocket a few times with his fist, and waited for the pitch. He took another deep breath.

Dad tossed him an underhand one, gently. Danny closed his eyes, turned his head away, and heard the ball thud to the grass. He looked back to find the ball resting by his feet.

"Almost! Good try!" said Dad. Ouch.

Across the grass, Walter was beginning to roll his eyes, but Dad caught him in the act. "Uh-uh," he cautioned, holding up a warning finger. Walter switched to an innocent face.

Dad's cell phone rang, and after peering at the display to see who the call was from, he reluctantly answered it. The boys weren't pleased.

"Yeah, Bill," they heard him say. "I'm not at my desk. I'll call you in five minutes." He hung up.

Danny tried using the moment to get out of playing baseball. "This game is stupid," he said. "Let's play Smash Brothers instead."

"Come on," Dad said. "You've been cooped up all day. It's nice to get out of the house."

Danny sighed heavily, picked up the ball, and threw it back to his father. It made it almost all the way there.

"Ready now? Watch the ball, not me," Dad said.

Danny nodded but kept staring at his father.

"The ball, Dan. Not me." Trying to lighten things up, he went into his sportscaster act: "There's a high fly ball to right field. Shawn Green heads back to the warning track . . ."

Dad tossed another underhand one, putting a little more heat on it. This one sailed higher. Danny looked up, raised his glove, and closed one eye. This time the ball actually hit his glove. He opened his eye in excitement just in time to see the ball bounce off his glove and fall behind him.

"And Milton Bradley with the diving snow cone!"

yelled Walter, flying in headfirst to catch it. "Dodgers win!" He rolled on the grass, holding the glove over his head to show off his spectacular snowcone grab.

Danny was furious. "Walter!" he hollered, hurling his glove into the dirt.

"DAAAAD!" Walter responded.

Dad tried to be judicious. "Danny—" he began.

"It's not fair!" Danny cut in. Then he stormed off across the yard and into the house.

Out in the yard, Dad sighed and looked at Walter. His expression said, Did you have to do that?

"What?" said Walter, all wounded innocence. "It was a great grab."

Meanwhile, Danny, having slammed the door behind him, stomped up the stairs to the second floor and down the hall. It was a big old house. True, it had seen better days, but with a little work it would be very comfortable and cozy.

Dad followed him into the house a few seconds later. "Danny?" he called.

No answer. He climbed the stairs to the second floor and headed down the hall toward the boys' bedroom at the end, but something made him stop as he passed the dumbwaiter.

The small wooden door to the dumbwaiter, at about waist height in the wall, was freckled with round holes. These were vents that let in light and air from the landing. It looked pretty much like a laundry chute, but behind the door there was actually a wooden box suspended from ropes. It worked like a little hand-operated elevator, and in the olden days it had been used for sending food and supplies up from the kitchen to the bedrooms above.

Danny's father pulled the door open abruptly. There was Danny inside, his knees pulled up to his chest and his thumb in his mouth. He whipped his thumb out of his mouth as soon as he saw his dad.

"You know you're not supposed to play in there," said Dad.

"I'm not playing. Playing is when you're having fun."

Dad squatted so he and Danny were at eye level. "You know, when I was six years old, I—"

"Six and three-quarters," Danny corrected him.

"When I was six and three-quarters, catching was hard for me too."

"It's not hard for Walter."

"Walter is nine," Dad said.

"So? He's still better. He's better than me at everything."

"You're getting good at the piano," Dad tried.

"I hate that stupid thing."

"Someday you'll be happy I got you a piano. You'll be at a party one day and there'll be a pretty girl—"

Sick of that old story, Danny launched himself out of the dumbwaiter and took off down the hall toward his room.

The walls of Danny and Walter's room were covered with posters. On Walter's side there were basketball players and athletes, and Danny's was heavy on fantasy illustrations. They had just moved in a couple of months ago, and not quite all the boxes were unpacked.

Danny flew into the room and threw himself on the bed face-down, with Dad not far behind.

"Look, Danny," said Dad, "you and Walter are different. He's good at some things, and you're good at some things. That's how people are."

"He beats me at everything."

"Listen to me, because this is important. You're a special kid, Danny."

"That's what people say when they can't think of anything," Danny said, sulking.

"You know how you always make up games and pretend to be characters and stuff? You have an incredible imagination."

Just outside the bedroom door, Walter lurked, listening to them and licking a Popsicle. "A great imagination," he heard Dad say to Danny. "A whole universe of an imagination. And, you know, I use my imagination for a living, so I know what I'm talking about."

In the bedroom, Danny sat up. "Is it better than Walter's?" he asked.

Walter stopped midlick, listening intently for the answer to that one.

"What?" said Dad, at a loss for words.

"Is my imagination better than Walter's?" Danny persisted.

Dad smiled and lowered his forehead against Danny's, as out in the hallway Walter leaned in closer, straining to hear.

"You're different from Walter," Dad whispered to Danny.

Walter was wild with frustration. He had not quite been able to make out his father's words, the most important ones.

"See?" Danny said. "I'm not better at anything." He flopped back down on the bed and faced away from his father.

Dad smiled. "You're not mad anymore—I can tell."

Danny sat up and looked at him. "I won't be mad if we play Smash Brothers."

Dad sighed. "I really want to play with you," he said, "but I can't right now. I have to make one phone call for work. There's a very important presentation today and I have to make sure everything's perfect."

"Okay, read to me." Danny thrust a book at Dad.

"I have to work."

Danny flopped back down dramatically.

Dad left the room and went down the stairs and into the living room. As soon as he got there, a football flew at his head. He managed to catch it. "Don't do that," he said.

Walter, who had thrown the football, sat in a chair facing the TV. It was tuned to his favorite show, *SportsCenter*. He had finished his Popsicle and was now drinking a big glass of red fruit punch. "Wanna play catch?" he asked his dad.

"We just did."

"No, football catch," said Walter.

"I have to work for an hour."

Walter was shocked. This was totally against the rules. "But it's Saturday!"

The phone rang in the other room. "Tell me about it," said Dad. He tossed the football back to Walter and walked into his office, which was a converted dining room. He plopped himself down at a big table, where an array of art supplies awaited him. He was working on an ad layout.

Walter appeared behind him, in the doorway. "All you ever do is work," he said.

"Nice try," said his dad. He answered the phone: "Hello?"

"This is so unfair," Walter grumbled.

"Hi," Dad said into the phone, ignoring Walter. "Yeah, I was just about to call you. Can you hang on just one second? Thanks." He covered the receiver and whispered to Walter, "I have a meeting this afternoon, Walter, and I have to be ready. Nothing I can do about it."

Now Walter was beyond shocked. "You're going *out?*"

"I'm going to a meeting. You'll already be at Mom's—she's picking you up at three."

Walter was confused. "We go to Mom's tomorrow."

"No, today." Dad spoke again into the phone: "Just one more second, okay?"

"But this is a four-day Dad week," Walter told him.

Dad spoke fast, needing to get back to his call. "No, three-day Dad week. Four-day last week, four-day next week, three-day this week. Four-day Mom's house this week."

Walter set his glass down dramatically. "That's not fair!"

Dad thought for a moment. "To whom?" he said.

"To anybody," said Walter.

Dad gave up and said into the phone, "Listen, Bill, I am so sorry. Two minutes. Thanks." He hung up and rolled his chair across the floor, gliding to a stop in front of Walter. He held his son by the arms. "Walter, I love you," he said. "And no, it isn't fair, to anyone. But I have to work."

Danny had come down the stairs and wandered over near the door to the office. Now it was his turn to lurk outside, listening.

"Ten throws," Walter wheedled.

"I have to work!"

"If Danny wasn't around, we'd have all the time we wanted," said Walter petulantly.

"Well, Danny is around," said Dad.

Danny leaned closer, outside the door, listening

hard. Almost unconsciously, he put his thumb back into his mouth.

"How about five throws?" Walter persisted. He threw the football to Dad, who caught it instinctively.

Now Dad was irritated. "I—how can I put this?—have to work," he said.

Danny appeared in the doorway, holding up two video game remotes, their cords dragging behind him.

"Dad, I'm ready for Smash Brothers," he said.

"*What?*" said Walter, injured to the core. "You told him you'd play Smash Brothers?"

"No, I didn't," said Dad. He threw the football back to Walter, to be done with it. He was attempting to keep his patience. Walter caught the ball and Danny pointed hysterically at this outrage.

"You're playing catch with Walter!"

Dad rubbed his head. "Guys . . . "

"He might, if you weren't here!" Walter yelled at his brother.

"YOU ARE SO MEAN!" Danny retorted. He looked up to God, somewhere in the direction of the ceiling. "EVERYBODY WANTS TO RUIN MY LIFE!" he said.

"Guys, please . . . " Dad begged.

"You never keep your promises!" Walter accused his father.

"ALL YOU CARE ABOUT IS WALTER!" Danny chimed in.

Dad finally snapped. "THERE'S ONLY ONE OF ME! Okay?" he yelled. "I don't like this situation either—it sucks, is what it does, but it's the best I could come up with, so climb off my back and give me about two inches of space, will you please?!"

They both just stared at him, wide-eyed. Walter set the football down on a bookcase, as if to apologize for pushing so hard. Danny dropped the remotes. He started to put his thumb in his mouth but caught himself and dropped his arms to his sides, his lower lip quivering.

They could see that Dad felt horrible. He sat back down and stared out the window, taking a breath to collect himself. Then he spoke softly, still facing away from them. "Do you boys remember the time I ate that bad chicken they keep under the lights at the supermarket," he said, "and I was sick all night, throwing up?"

They nodded.

"And the next morning," he went on, "we had to get on the plane to go to Grandma's, and Lisa and Mom were away and I was still so sick I could barely stand up?"

He turned around and faced them so they would really pay attention.

"Remember before we left, when I told you guys I needed you to grow up a few years, right then in that very moment, so that you could help me on the trip instead of me helping you? Otherwise we wouldn't make it?"

They kept nodding.

"Remember what happened?"

Danny and Walter looked at each other.

"We grew up?" Danny guessed.

Now Dad nodded. "There are some days, guys, when you gotta grow up all at once. I need today to be one of those days."

They got it. They didn't like it, but they got it.

In thirty seconds flat the two brothers had retreated to their room, slammed the door, and flopped down on their beds. They were bored. They were mad. But they were going to let Dad work.

Neither one said anything for a while. Then Danny said, "Do you want to play Chutes and Ladders?"

"No. You'll cheat."

"Stratego?" Danny tried.

"No. You cheat at board games."

"But you can't even cheat at Stratego!"

Walter just ignored him.

Downstairs, Dad dropped back into his office chair and rubbed his face with his hands, trying to get his focus back. Then he picked up the phone and dialed. "Hi," he said. "Sorry about that." He listened to the voice on the other end. "No no, it's fine. I'm not meeting him till three-thirty; I can finish by then."

Danny, in the bedroom, began rummaging through a toy chest, tossing out boring stuff, looking for good stuff. He came up with two very fancy, high-tech walkie-talkies. He turned one on and static came out.

"Excuse me," Walter said, "could you please put those back right now this minute? They belong to me."

"You never play with them."

"They're still mine."

"When did you get so mean?" said Danny.

"I'm not mean, Danny. I'm in third grade. I have a girlfriend. You know how Dad said we have to grow up? Well, this is what it looks like."

Danny held out one of the walkie-talkies invitingly.

Downstairs, Dad was shuffling through the layout materials on his desk, talking on the phone. "The drawings all match the clay mockup," he was saying. There was an angry shriek from upstairs. He looked up at the ceiling. "Yes. Red," he continued, trying to block out the disturbance.

Then he heard the boys' bedroom door bang open. "DAAAAAAD!" yowled Walter. The next sound was feet thudding on the stairs.

Dad knew that all heck was about to break loose, so he tried to wrap his conversation up fast. "Cranberry. Right. It's whatever color they picked. I worked from the chits. Uh, can I call you back one more time real quick? Small domestic emergency here. No, I know. I know. Not a problem. Okay. Okay. Thanks."

He hung up the phone just as the door to his office burst open. There was Walter, holding one of his walkie-talkies in his hand. He displayed its newly broken antenna as if he were a prosecutor showing a murder weapon.

"Look what he did!" Walter said.

Dad tried to sound calm. "I was on the phone," he said.

Walter just kept going. "He breaks everything!"

Now Danny was behind him in the doorway, hands shoved in pockets, looking ashamed.

Both boys talked at once, presenting their cases.

"It was an accident . . . " Danny said.

"He is such a baby!" said Walter.

"Walter—" Dad tried interrupting. Nobody listened to him.

"I'm NOT a baby!" said Danny.

"He breaks all my stuff," said Walter.

". . . said it was an accident . . . " Danny repeated.

"—he can't catch a ball—" Walter went on.

"That's enough," Dad warned.

Walter now whirled on Danny to drive his point home: "And nobody wants you around!"

"YOU SHUT UP!" Danny yelled. Enraged, he grabbed Walter's football from the bookcase next to the door and hurled it at Walter's head as hard as he could. Walter ducked.

Dad's eyes popped open very wide, and he lunged for it—but the ball sailed past his outstretched fingertips, smacked into the glass of red fruit punch Walter had left on the desk, and spilled all over the layout. Dad leaped to his feet.

Walter gasped.

Danny's face turned white.

"I'm sorry!" Danny cried.

There was no reply.

"I'm sorry I'm sorry I'm sorry I'm sorry I'm sorry I'm sorry!"

Dad said nothing. He just stared down at the desk, defeated, as the ruby red fruit drink seeped into all his work.

Five minutes later, Walter and Danny sat next to each other in the middle of the couch, watching guiltily as Dad pulled on his jacket, got his wallet and keys, and headed for the front door.

"It's ten minutes to the office," he said. "I just have to go to the art department and run off another copy and I'll be right back."

"You're gonna leave us alone in this creepy old house?" Danny said.

"It's not creepy, it's just old," Dad replied.

"I like Mom's house better," said Walter.

"Well, so did she, and now it's hers," said Dad, catching himself as he realized how much bitterness had crept into his tone. "Look," he went on more gently, "this house is a very special house. And the reason I've been working so hard to fix it up is that I want to make a home for us here. Now I know it's not like Mom's house, and I know it's a little creaky, but give it some time. It's gonna grow on you."

"Well, I don't want to stay here alone," said Danny.

Dad glanced up the stairs. "You won't be. I'll wake Lisa."

Danny and Walter began to howl together: "*NOOO!*" and "Are you *crazy?*"

But it was too late. Dad was already opening Lisa's door.

Lisa was sixteen, pretty, and snappish, even while sleeping. Which she was right now. Only a fool would wake her up.

"Honey," whispered Dad. "Lisa, wake up."

Lisa rolled over and looked at him through one open eye. "Go away," she said.

"I need you to look after the kids," he said.

"I can't."

"Get up."

"I need to crash a little longer."

"You've been asleep for fourteen hours," Dad pointed out.

"What time is it?" she asked groggily.

"Two."

"In the afternoon?"

"Yeah."

"What day?"

"Saturday."

"So why are you waking me up?" she demanded.

"I have to go out. I need you to watch your two favorite people in the world."

Lisa was indignant. "You promised I'd never have to do that again."

"I would never make that promise," he said.

"I can't help you. I have a date."

"What time?"

"We're hooking up at eight."

"It's *two,*" said Dad.

"So?"

"That's six hours from now."

"What's your point?"

"My point is, I need you to look after the boys. And it makes me really uncomfortable," he added, "when you say 'hooking up.'"

"Why? It's not like it means anything."

"I hope it doesn't," he said.

"It doesn't. It's just an expression."

"I hope it is."

"It is. God. We should have never rented *Thirteen.*"

Dad sighed. "Just keep an eye on them and make sure they don't set the place on fire. Okay?"

There was no reply. "Okay?" he repeated.

"I'm not deaf," she said.

"Huh?" he joked.

Lisa was not amused. "Fine. Fifteen minutes! Close the door!"

He walked out, and Lisa got out of bed to close her door. Looking out the window, she watched her father come out the front door below and walk toward his car, speaking on the cell phone. She yawned and yanked the drapes shut. Then she grabbed her CD player, turned it up, and put on her headphones and a sleep shade. She dived back under the covers, rolled over, and faced the wall.

Which left Danny and Walter alone in the living room, if you didn't count Danny's gerbil, Richard, in the cage on the floor.

Danny turned on the TV and began playing a video game. Immediately, Walter walked over to the game and turned it off.

"Hey!" Danny said.

"Dad said no video games," Walter told him.

"He did not!" Danny paused, knowing he was going to lose this one. "Fine," he said. He switched the channel and the TV came on, showing an episode of *SpongeBob SquarePants.*

SpongeBob, as usual, was frustrated by Mr. Crabs. "Tartar sauce!" he sputtered.

Walter grabbed the remote and flicked it over to *SportsCenter.*

"Hey! I was watching that!" Danny protested.

In response, Walter held the remote out and turned up the volume. Danny sighed. "Can't we watch *SpongeBob?*" he said.

"No."

"You *used* to like it."

"Times change," said Walter coldly.

"Tartar sauce," Danny muttered.

Walter kept watching *SportsCenter* while Danny considered how to get his brother's attention. "I'm hungry," he finally said.

"What do you want me to do about it?" asked Walter.

"Make me some macaroni and cheese?"

"I don't know how."

"I'm hungry," Danny repeated. "What do you know how to make?"

"Water."

Danny thought for a moment and then left the room. He came back a few seconds later with two baseball gloves and a ball, and dropped them on the floor in front of him. He stood there, hoping Walter would notice. Walter, however, carefully ignored him.

"How 'bout if you and me play catch?" Danny asked.

"You and I," Walter corrected, not taking his eyes off the television. "And no."

Danny still stood there, frustrated, waiting for Walter to look at him. But Walter refused.

Now Danny picked up the ball and tossed it gently into the chair next to Walter. Never taking his eyes off the TV, Walter picked it up and dropped it on the carpet, rolling it almost back to Danny in a most uncatchlike manner.

Undeterred, Danny picked it up and tossed it again, a little bit harder. Walter saw it coming and took his eyes off the tube just long enough to catch it. Again, he dropped it on the carpet.

Danny marched forward, picked it up again, and went back to where he'd been standing. He looked at Walter, stymied.

Walter just stared at the TV, his eyes glazing over—until the baseball hit him on the head. "OW!" he yelled.

"I'M SORRY I'M SORRY I'M SORRY I'M SORRY!" cried Danny, who hadn't exactly meant to hit him on the head.

"You're DEAD!" Walter shouted.

Danny took off, and Walter bolted out of the chair and after him. They raced through the den and the kitchen and up the back stairs. Danny took them two at a time, but Walter was able to cover them three at a time. He was closing in.

Danny ran into their bedroom and slammed the door behind him. There was no lock, so he pushed against it as hard as he could. But Walter was right behind him, pushing on the other side of the door.

"Open up, Danny!" he yelled. "You're only making it worse!"

He was shoving, and Danny was shoving back, but it was a losing battle. Walter was stronger and heavier. The door was starting to come open.

So Danny jumped back, hiding behind the door as

it flew open. Walter tumbled into the room as Danny raced around the door and out into the hallway, leaving Walter to scramble to his feet and chase after his brother.

Walter raced into the hallway. No Danny. That was weird. How could he have gone all the way down the hall so fast?

Inside the dumbwaiter, Danny was curled up in a ball, knees to his chest, trying not to breathe hard. Through the vent holes in the wooden door, he could see the hallway outside. Walter was approaching.

"*Daaaaannnnyyyy,*" he said in a scary, singsong horror-movie voice.

Danny held his breath as Walter drew closer.

"Don't worry, Danny. I'm not going to hurt you."

Danny finally exhaled as Walter walked right past.

Walter's voice faded as he continued down the hall. "I'm only going to . . ." The door of the dumbwaiter suddenly flew open and Walter's face loomed right in front of Danny's, grinning with malicious glee.

"KILL YOU!" crowed Walter.

Danny screamed. He tried to get out of the dumbwaiter, but Walter slammed the door on him. Danny pushed against it, but Walter pushed back, trapping him there.

"You're a jerk!" Danny yelled, panting from the struggle.

"You're a dwarf!" Walter rejoined.

"Why are you so mean to me?" Danny wailed. "You're supposed to be my brother!"

"You'll be safe in here till Dad gets back," Walter said with a snicker.

"You're just jealous 'cause Dad thinks I'm smarter than you!"

Eyes gleaming with mischief, Walter spied the rope that hung alongside the dumbwaiter. The rope was stretched tight, looped around a pulley that was fastened to the wall. Walter grabbed hold of the rope and started pulling down on it, hand over hand. The wooden box started to descend.

"NO! DON'T!" screamed Danny.

But he was already out of sight, as Walter hauled on the rope like a madman, lowering Danny down, down, down . . .

"Walter! DON'T! DON'T! PULL ME UP! PULL ME UP!" Danny shrieked in true terror.

"What's the matter, Danny? You're not still scared of the *basement,* are you?" said Walter in his creepy voice.

Danny had never been in the dumbwaiter when it was going down the shaft. It was much darker than it was upstairs. The thing jiggled and rocked as it dropped toward the basement.

"WAAAAALLLLTERRR!" he screamed again.

Walter leaned his head in from above and shouted

down at Danny. "Three-year-olds are scared of basements!" he taunted.

Neither one of them could see the dumbwaiter pulley straining at the deteriorating joist to which it was anchored.

The dumbwaiter clunked to a halt, leaving Danny stuck in almost total darkness. He was frozen, his eyes wide. "Walter? Pull me up, Walter!" he managed to croak.

Walter slammed the door and headed back downstairs.

In the dumbwaiter, Danny crouched, trembling and panicky. He peered through the holes in the door but couldn't see much. After a while, he gathered all his courage, touched the door, and pushed it open *eeeeeee*ver so slightly. His eyes peeked around the edge of the slightly open door. The only light coming into the basement was from a few wayward beams that filtered through the crack in the storm cellar doors—not nearly enough to light the whole creepy place.

And it was creepy too. It appeared that they had inherited a bunch of junk from sixty or seventy years' worth of previous owners who didn't feel like clearing it out. There was stuff piled everywhere.

Danny pushed the door open a teensy bit more, took a deep breath, and hurled himself out of the dumbwaiter. He hit the floor running, heading for a closed door at the far end. When he reached it, he threw the door open, revealing a stairwell that led upstairs. He lunged inside, tripping on the steps and landing so hard on his stomach that it nearly knocked the wind out of him.

Wriggling around, he managed to slam the door behind him. Quickly he flicked the deadbolt lock on the basement door.

Whew. He lay there, crumpled at the bottom of the steps, breathing heavily. He was safe for the time being.

But as he started to get up, he stopped, his curiosity aroused. There was something under one of the stairs. It looked as if it had been shoved there a long, long time ago. You would never have seen it unless you had fallen at the bottom of the steps, just the way Danny had.

It was a tattered old cardboard box, and it looked like it had to be about fifty years old. Letters on the edge of the box read

ZATHURA
A Space Adventure

Danny pulled the box out and admired it. Even if it was old, it looked pretty cool.

He put it under his arm and went up the stairs.

In the living room, Walter was slumped in the chair in front of the television, watching his show again. Danny came into the living room with the box and a scowl for Walter. "You're mean," Danny said.

"You're a midget," said Walter.

And that about summed up their positions. No further conversation was necessary.

Danny dropped cross-legged onto the carpet by the window and looked at his treasure. The cover of the box was decorated with space stuff, like old-fashioned rockets and star fields. He opened it.

The game was made of pressed metal, its design decidedly antique. Everything was well worn. On the inside of the box in large letters it said, "The Rules," but naturally Danny didn't bother reading them.

"Check out what I found in the basement," he said to Walter.

Walter craned around from his chair and looked at the game, a bored expression on his face. "Looks dumb and old," he said.

"I like it," said Danny.

"You would. It's for babies." He turned back to the TV.

Danny frowned and looked back at the board. It was a star field, like on the front of the box, with a path of colored circles that led to a large black planet labeled "Zathura." There were no dice. Instead, there was a skate key that wound up a crank, and a spinning number dial next to it.

Danny looked at the game pieces, which were different-colored rocket ships. There was a red ship and a blue ship that traveled along in a mechanical track that started on the planet Earth.

"First one to the black planet wins, I guess," said Danny. "Will you play with me?"

"No" was Walter's predictable response. His eyes were glued to the TV.

"I won't cheat," Danny promised.

"Yes, you will."

Danny sighed and looked at the board again. Earth looked like the starting spot. He cranked the skate key, punched the button, and the number tumbler spun, stopping on a five. Danny reached out to move one of the rocket ships, but the red ship started moving all by itself, ka-chunking ahead four spaces. Richard the gerbil watched the piece move.

"Cool! Walter, check this out."

When the ship reached the fourth square, a

buzzing sound came from the board. Danny's eyes widened as, with a smart little click, a small white card popped out of the edge of the board right in front of him.

"A card came out!" Danny said excitedly.

"Fascinating," said Walter. He did not even turn to look.

Danny took the card and studied it. It had a big *Z* on one side and words on the other. Danny furrowed his brow as he tried reading it: "'Meet . . . meaty . . . meetor shoe . . . meat or shoe . . .'"

Walter found his view of the television suddenly blocked by Danny's face. "Read this for me?" Danny asked.

Walter sighed and took the card from Danny. "'Meteor shower: take evasive action,'" he read.

"What's 'evasive action'?" asked Danny.

"It's when you get out of the way of something."

Danny looked around and took one step to the side. He looked around again. "What exactly am I supposed to get out of the way of, exactly?" he asked.

"I don't know . . . all it says is—"

He looked back at the card for further information, but stopped midsentence. There was a small, smoking hole right in the middle of the card. "Huh?" he said. He bent down and peered more closely at the hole. Through it, he could see another hole, also small and also smoking, in the floor between his feet.

He looked up and saw a matching hole in the ceiling directly above the card.

"Oh . . . wow," said Walter.

There was a sudden roar of white noise as the TV went to snow. Then, up above them, they heard a *rat-a-tat* sound on the roof.

"It's a hailstorm!" said Walter.

*Poink!* A rock dropped onto the floor in front of them.

*Ssssss!* The rock burned a hole in the floor, then dropped through the living room and fell into the basement below.

Walter and Danny looked at each other.

*Teenk!* A meteor smashed a vase on an end table.

*Thwok!* A meteor ripped through the seat of a side chair.

*Boom!* A meteor popped next to the gerbil cage.

*Krak!* A meteor broke an urn of ashes on the mantel.

*Pow!* A meteor smashed through a pile of books on a shelf.

"It's not hail!" Danny yelled. He grabbed the card and waved it in front of him. "IT'S METEORS!"

*Tak! Tak! Tak! Tak!* The drizzle of meteors increased to a shower, and then—

*BAMBAMBAMBAMBAMBAMBAM!* There was a furious pounding, like a thousand golf balls hammering down on them. Danny and Walter shouted to each other, but their words were lost in the cacophony.

"TAKE ERASIVE ACTION, TAKE ERASIVE ACTION!" Danny hollered. Then he proceeded to do his version of that, which was to run around in circles.

Up in Lisa's room, the muffled screams of her brothers were audible. But Lisa was in the isolation tank, sleep shade on, headphones blaring. Still, she must have sensed the noise, because she reached down, spun the wheel on her MP3 player, and cranked the music even louder.

In the living room, a softball-size meteor smashed through the ceiling, blasted right through the coffee table in front of Danny, and crunched through the floor below it, burrowing deep out of sight. Danny leaped back. One golf-ball-size meteor after another smashed through the ceiling and cratered into the floor. No matter where he went, they seemed to be landing right behind Danny.

The gerbil nervously paced in his cage as meteors careened all around him, just missing the glass.

Walter, meanwhile, was running across the living room, pursued by crashing meteors, which nipped at his heels. He raced into the sanctuary of the fireplace. Watching Danny do all he could to avoid the deadly storm, he called out to his brother from the safety of the hearth, "Danny! In here!"

Danny grabbed the gerbil cage and made his way to the fireplace, crouching down beside his brother.

Slowly the meteors tapered off. The two brothers watched in awe as the last of the projectiles plinked to the floor.

There was silence for a second. They looked at the smoking, smashed, ruined living room.

The TV flashed back to life. *SportsCenter* was back on.

They crept out of the hearth and examined the trashed room.

Danny saw that the gerbil had survived.

"I don't think we should play—" Danny started saying, just as a huge meteor, six feet across, smashed through the roof.

The meteor plummeted downward into the house at an angle and smashed through the wall that divided the living room from the foyer. Danny and Walter leaped out of the way as it pulverized the television.

"Holy sh—" Walter started saying.

Danny cut him off. "Tartar sauce!"

Walter and Danny slowly got to their feet and walked over to either side of the crater it had left. Then everything went quiet again. The meteor shower had stopped. The dust began to settle.

"Told you," said Danny finally. "Meteors."

In shock, Walter looked down at the giant meteor that was now buried in their floor. He looked up, through holes in two walls, through the jagged hole in the roof. Outside, there was a night sky, brilliantly dotted with starlight. "Dad is gonna kill us!" he said. "He just sanded the floors."

Slowly, he and Danny crossed to the foyer to further inspect the hole in the roof. When they looked down, they noticed that the meteor damage abruptly ended at the living room threshold. It was clear that the meteor storm had hit only one room.

"Weird," said Walter.

Danny looked up through the roof and gazed at the endless black sky and the dazzling star field. "Wow. Outer space," he said.

Walter shook his head. "It's not outer space, Danny. It's nighttime."

"I don't know, Walter. Night never looked so . . . close before."

They both turned and looked at the front door. Danny walked toward it, but Walter did not. He just watched his brother.

Slowly, Danny opened the door. He peeked outside, then turned back to Walter, amazed. "Walter. Come here," he said.

Danny swung the front door all the way open, and he and Walter stepped out onto the front porch. But the odd thing was, there was no outside there anymore. At least, not the one they expected. It was as if the front porch opened up directly on the outer reaches of the solar system. It looked like the view from the windshield of a spaceship, if spaceships had such things.

In fact, if Danny and Walter had been able to see the house from a distance, they would have seen that it was completely detached from its earthly moorings, trailing pipes and power wires out its basement. It looked like a molar that had been ripped out by the roots. Saturn was clearly visible up ahead, its icy, brilliantly colored rings lit up like a billion jewels. Walter's bike, which had been parked on the front porch, drifted lazily alongside the house.

Cautiously, Danny and Walter walked to the edge of the porch. They looked up. Amazing. They looked down. Incredible.

Being a boy, Walter did the natural thing: he hacked a gob of spit out off the edge of the porch to see what would happen.

It floated lazily away.

The boys backed up carefully to the front door, stepped back inside, and closed the door softly behind them. Walter turned and looked at the wrecked living room with fresh awe. "We gotta call Dad!" he said, grabbing the phone. Of course, there was no dial tone.

"It doesn't work!" he said.

"Well, duh," said Danny.

"Danny, there's only one thing to do, and I know you're not gonna like it, but we have to wake Lisa."

"No no no!"

But of course, it had to be yes yes yes. Even she would have to agree that this was serious.

The boys hesitantly walked into Lisa's darkened bedroom and stood over her. Walter was clutching the Zathura game. "Tell her," he said to Danny.

"You tell her," said Danny.

"You should tell her," Walter said. "She won't freak out as much."

"We shouldn't even really be in here."

"I think, under the circumstances, she'll understand."

"Then you wake her," Danny said.

"Fine." Walter bent over and whispered into the Ear of Doom. "Lisa . . . Lisa . . ."

Lisa did not even open her eyes. "Go away," she mumbled.

"Lisa . . . " Walter tried again.

She half opened one eye. "What is the rule about being in my room?" she demanded.

"We're not allowed in unless it's an emergency," the two of them recited together.

"So what's the emergency?"

Now both of them gushed out the story, talking fast at the same time.

"We started playing this board game and it turned real and sent us into outer space and we don't know how to—" Danny said.

"There was a meteor shower and everything got wrecked and now we're in space and we don't know how to—" Walter said.

"—get back to Earth!" they finished as one.

"Quiet!" Lisa yelled above their urgent pleas.

Walter pulled open the curtains to reveal the stars and darkness of outer space. "Just look!" he cried.

Lisa sat up, gravely concerned. "Oh, no!" she said.

"Yes!" they both cried, relieved that help was finally on the way. "What do we do?"

But Lisa, unfortunately, was not reacting to what they had said at all. She was looking past them at the blackness outside. "It's dark already! I'm gonna be late!" she said, leaping up and sprinting for the bathroom.

"It's *not* dark already!" Danny said.

"We're in outer space!" Walter said at the same time.

She slammed the bathroom door in their faces, and they pounded on it frantically. Finally the door opened and Lisa poked her head out. The bathroom was filling with steam. "Just shut up and listen to me," she told them. "Dad left me in charge until he gets home. That means you gotta do what I say. Do me a favor: go downstairs and just stay out of my face."

"It's an emergency!" Walter wailed.

Lisa was unsympathetic. "Is anyone hurt?" she said.

"No," Walter had to admit.

"Is the house on fire?"

"No. But . . ."

"Then leave."

"Lisa. Please," Danny begged her. "We're really scared. Can you just watch what this game does?"

"If this is some kind of weird joke," she warned, "I swear to God you're dead."

Nervously, Danny spun the wheel. "Watch out! Here it comes!" he told Lisa.

"Protect yourself!" Walter said.

The wheel stopped on nine, and Walter's spaceship thunked forward nine spaces. The board buzzed and spat out a card.

"Hang on," said Danny. "The card's the scary part."

Walter took the card and read it. "'You are promoted to Starship Captain,'" he read. "'Move ahead two spaces.'"

They both cowered in anticipation. The piece plinked ahead two spaces.

"Fascinating," said Lisa. And then she was gone, slamming and locking the bathroom door behind her. The music came back on.

"No! Wait!" Danny called after her.

"Just go, hurry up!" Walter said to him. He shouted into the bathroom, "Hang on, Lisa, that one didn't count—I'll spin again."

It didn't move.

"It's stuck!" Walter said.

"Let me try," said Danny. He pushed it, and this time it spun. It was a four. "I guess you gotta take turns," he said.

*BUZZ.* A card popped out. Danny took it as Walter leaned in over his shoulder. "'Shipmate enters cryonic sleep chamber for five turns,'" he read.

"What the heck does that mean?" Danny asked him.

All of a sudden, the sound of the shower stopped from behind the bathroom door. The music stopped too. Worried, Danny and Walter looked at each other.

"Lisa?" said Walter.

They noticed that steam was no longer coming from under the door of the bathroom. In fact, there was a thin seam of ice along the bottom now. The frost quickly spread from there to cover the whole door.

"Does 'cryonic' mean 'ice'?" Danny asked.

Walter got up and tried to open the door, but it was frozen shut. "Help me!" he said.

He and Danny lowered their shoulders and ran full tilt into the door, which gave way.

It was cold in the bathroom—really, really cold. The room was now in a deep freeze. The tub was an ice rink, and the steam that hung in the air was more like hail and fell when you touched it. The water that was coming out of the showerhead was frozen in long strands, as if someone had stopped time.

Lisa stood frozen in her bathrobe, her hair white with frost, one hand outstretched amid the frozen strands. She must have been feeling the shower water before jumping in.

"I killed her!" Danny bawled.

"No, you didn't—she's just frozen in cryonic sleep!" Walter said. "We gotta melt her." He turned and ran out of the room.

Danny slowly approached the eerie sight of his ice sculpture sister.

In a minute, Walter rushed back in with a can of hair spray and a lighter. He aimed the hair spray into the flame, which had the effect of creating a huge blowtorch. He pointed the fire at Lisa.

"ARE YOU CRAZY?!" yelled Danny.

He knocked the hair spray out of Walter's hand and the flame immediately went out.

"We can't just leave her like this!" said Walter.

"You shouldn't even be doing that!" Danny said.

"Well, we gotta do something. What did the rules say?"

"I didn't read them."

That stopped Walter cold. It was definitely time to give the rules a read.

In seconds, they were back in the smashed-up living room, sitting cross-legged on either side of the game board. Walter was holding up the box top and reading aloud the words that were printed on the inside: "'Attention all Space Rangers: Zathura awaits! Do you have what it takes to navigate the galaxy? It's not for the faint of heart, for once you embark upon your journey there is no turning back until Zathura is reached. Pieces reset at the end of each game. Play again and again for different adventures.' That's it. We gotta keep playing."

Danny shook his head. "I'm not playing that thing!"

"We have to. It says we get home if we play."

"It didn't say that."

"'Pieces reset at the end of each game.' That means we go home when we finish."

"Alls I know is when we play that game, bad things happen."

"*All* I know," said Walter, "is when I went, I got promoted. I'm gonna win this thing and get home." He started winding up the skate key.

"Wait . . ."

"Don't be a baby." Walter hit the button. The spinner spun, slowing to a stop. "Eight. Look, I'm halfway there," he said with satisfaction. Walter reached out to move his ship. But like before, the board took over—

whirring and clicking as it moved his rocket ahead eight spaces. It landed on a blue circle.

The board buzzed and a card popped out in front of him. Walter took it. He held his breath and moved it slowly up in front of his eyes, cradled it in the palm of his hand, looked at the words . . . and screamed at the top of his lungs!

Danny leaped to his feet. "WHAT WHAT WHAT?!" he yelled.

Walter grinned. "I'm just yankin' ya," he said, chuckling.

"You are so not hilarious," said Danny, sitting back down. "What does it say?"

Walter read it out loud: "'Your robot is defective.'"

"What does that mean?"

"It means my robot is broken."

"But you don't even have a robot," Danny said.

From the hallway outside came the sound of rattling metal and a steady *clank, clank, clank*. Both boys jumped up, looking for the source of the sound. A shadow fell on the floor in the hallway, growing larger. It was a very scary shadow, all gigantic arms and claws, and it was steadily growing. Now the shadow completely filled the hallway outside the door. This thing had to be absolutely . . .

Well, turned out it was tiny. A shiny metal robot about a foot tall walked into the doorway and stopped.

"That's your robot?" Danny said, looking down at it.

"At least I got one."

The robot's upper body rotated toward them. Its eyes lit up, and faint red search beams came on and scanned the room. The beams passed over Danny, but then they fell on Walter and stopped. They were fixed on the card he still held in his hands.

"What does it do?" Danny wanted to know.

"Anything I want." Walter turned to the little robot. "Get me a juice box."

The robot did not respond or react.

"Don't do that," said Danny, fretting.

"Why not? It's my robot."

"You might get it mad."

"It's three inches tall. I'll punt it across the room. It's my robot. The card says."

"I never said it wasn't yours. You don't have to be an idiot."

"You're just jealous 'cause you don't have one," Walter said.

Over by the doorway, unbeknownst to the arguing kids, the robot seemed to be getting larger.

"EMERGENCY," it said.

Walter and Danny wheeled around in time to see the robot begin to grow faster. Its lower section extended, its arms telescoped out, twenty-four additional layers of metal shielding whip-whap-whipped around its midsection, and its head quadrupled in size. Whole metal sections were unfurling from within the thing.

"No, no!" Walter ordered without effect.

"EMERGENCY," repeated the robot.

"No, it isn't!" said Walter. He dropped the card as if it were on fire. "There's no emergency!"

"ALIEN LIFE FORM. ALIEN LIFE FORM," said the robot.

"Walter, he's talking about you," said Danny.

"MUST DESTROY," said the robot. It had now reached its full size, standing six feet tall and four feet wide. Its clawlike hands extended and snapped open and shut several times quickly, and the red beams from its eyes locked in on Walter.

"RUN!" yelled Danny.

They bolted in opposite directions just as twin turbo jets emerged from the robot's back. The jets spat blue flame, and the robot's legs folded up behind it as it rocketed across the floor toward Walter. He lunged out of the way just in time, and the robot smashed into the wall behind where he'd been standing. Rubble and plaster fell around the gerbil cage in the fireplace.

The robot's head pivoted around and looked at Walter, but its body stayed where it was, driven completely into the wall and stuck there.

"ALIEN INVASION. MUST DESTROY," said the robot.

Walter stared, wide-eyed. "Roll, Danny," he said quietly.

"It's okay!" said Danny, in huge relief. "It's stuck!"

But the robot was working on that. Its right arm snaked around to its back and flipped open a circular panel there. The claw-hand snapped into the center of the circular panel and came out spinning, now attached to—eeek!—a circular saw.

"Danny, GO! IT'S YOUR TURN!" Walter screamed.

"I'm scared," Danny dithered.

The robot, meanwhile, used the saw to free itself from the wall and wheeled to face Walter, who pelted across the room toward the open door to the den.

In the living room, Danny slid to the floor in front of the game board and stared down at it. He was too scared to actually take his turn.

Walter, meanwhile, ran across the hall from the den to the kitchen, followed by the rocketing robot.

"Danny!" he yelled at the top of his lungs. He ran into Dad's office, but the broad shoulders of the mechanical monster smashed through two door frames as the robot came after him.

In the living room, Danny was a wreck, paralyzed with fear. He could hear the sound of walls and furniture being destroyed. It was echoing through the halls.

Finally, Walter raced out of the dining room, pursued by the robot. Walter leaped, but he hooked a foot on the back of the couch and went sprawling to the floor—just as the robot blasted through the air right over him. It smashed through one of the picture windows, its blue jets fading as it disappeared into the blackness of space.

Walter limped back to the living room, where he and Danny looked at each other, breathing hard. "Why didn't you push the button?" Walter said. "I coulda been killed!"

"I got scared. What's the big deal? He's gone, isn't he?"

But no, he wasn't. The robot smashed back into the house through the other plate-glass window, narrowly missing Walter and plowing into the wall across the house on the far end of the dining room.

The boys screamed. Danny dropped to his knees in front of the game board and started to fumble with the key to wind it up. Walter stared at the robot, fifty feet away. It was rising to its massive metal feet.

"Push the button . . . " Walter said from between clenched teeth.

Danny wound the key furiously. "I'm trying."

The robot shook off the hit it had taken and squared off at Walter. Its eyes beamed red and its saw spun in anticipation.

"Push the button . . ." said Walter.

Danny smacked the button for the spinner. The wheel spun, he got a seven, and his ship started moving.

The robot shifted its weight as steam blew from its nostrils. It slowly stepped forward.

"PUSH THE BUTTON!" Walter yelled.

"I did," Danny said. "It's still moving."

The game board buzzed and spat out a card. Walter snatched Danny's card and ran out of the room to the den. The robot veered right toward the kitchen in an attempt to head him off in the back.

The house shuddered and seemed to tilt. Walter lost his balance momentarily but managed to brace himself in the doorway as he read the card:

YOU PASS TOO CLOSE TO TSOURIS-3
GRAVITY INCREASED.

In the living room, the game board slowly began to slide toward the window of its own accord. The curve of an immense, glowing planet peeked through the window. It was Tsouris-3.

"What's it say?" Danny called to Walter.

Now Danny started to slide toward the window, sucked there by some invisible force. He backed up to fight the pull of gravity, but it was really, really strong. The room was awash with the orange light of the huge gas giant. The orange planet was so dense that they could hear it humming.

Walter was wedged in the door frame, fighting the gravitational pull. Just then, the robot appeared, precariously negotiating the slippery floor. It closed in on Walter from the hallway.

Upstairs in the hallway, the piano, pulled by the force of the planet's gravity, rolled into the stairway railing and broke almost all the way through it. It stopped, hanging slightly off the edge.

Danny stood in the center of the living room as the gravity got more powerful. The curtains began to rise toward the window. The plants bent. The chandelier rocked upward. Books flew through the air. Danny began to pitch at an angle to compensate for the planet's pull. With enormous effort, he managed to reach the far wall and grab a sconce. But the pull was so strong that his feet left the ground and the lighting fixture began to give from its mounting bracket.

Walter was now braced almost sideways in the doorway. The robot was all but prone as it attempted to slash Walter with its saw-blade hand. It used the closed basement door as a platform from which it could almost reach the boy. The blade chewed deep gashes into the hardwood floor, just inches from Walter's feet.

Meanwhile, Lisa, up in her bathroom, was still

frozen. But the gravitational pull was working on her too. Her frozen hand snapped free of the frozen shower stream, and her feet began to break loose.

Downstairs, Danny hung on for dear life as he teetered on the brink of disaster, close to falling across the living room into the window separating him from Tsouris-3. The sconce mounting gave way, and now he was hanging from the wiring. Then the wiring pulled through a length of plaster and finally released Danny into a free fall toward the picture window. He landed face-first into the plate glass, which, miraculously, didn't break.

A lamp smashed through the windowpane beside him and tumbled out into space.

Frozen Lisa slid with alarming speed through the wedged-open bathroom door and into her bedroom. Her bed had been upended by gravity, and all her things had collected against the wall. She smacked into the growing pile of stuff.

Walter sat perched atop the door frame, the robot snapping at his heels with its left claw-hand. Walter was just beyond its reach. But he was not safe for long. The robot coiled itself and sprang the six inches it took in order to grab hold of Walter's left sneaker, pulling the boy to certain doom.

The sheer mass of the robot, however, was enough to break through the basement door when it landed, sending the huge behemoth tumbling down the stairwell in an unceremonious heap.

Walter, in turn, was flung down the hallway by the momentum of the robot's fall. He rolled down the long hallway like a bowling ball down an alley and slammed into the oak front door with a hollow thud. His sneaker was long gone.

Outside, the huge orange planet began to pull away. Danny slid down the window. In the fireplace, the gerbil in the wheel returned to his normal position. The branches on the ficus plant slowly rose again as the planet released its grip.

Danny thumped to the floor, dropping off the window as the planet released its hold on him.

Still frozen, Lisa slid into Walter against the front door.

"Uhhhhhh," Walter gasped.

"Walter?" Danny called.

"It's Lisa," said Walter.

"Is she awake?"

Walter got up from a pile of debris collected in the entryway and stared at her. "I hope not," he said. "Lisa?"

Danny came to join him and found Walter knocking on her rigid, frozen frame. "Holy cow! Is she okay?" he said.

"She's in one piece," said Walter.

"What happened to the robot?" Danny asked.

That question could only be answered by taking a look. Cautiously, Walter and Danny stood at the top of the basement stairs and looked down. They stared in shock at the pile of broken robot that lay face-up in a pool of black oil. The saw-blade arm was firmly planted in the robot's own chest. Walter's sneaker sat on its lifeless breastplate. Walter slowly crept down the creaky stairs.

*"What are you doing?"* Danny whispered.

"I think it's dead," said Walter.

Danny was not so sure. "Let's just lock the door," he said.

Walter delicately snatched his sneaker. This emboldened him. He leaned over and peered into the robot's eyes, which no longer glowed red; they were a dead black. It didn't move. He even went as far as giving it a little kick.

*"Get up here!"* Danny whispered.

"I'm telling you, he's dea—" Walter was cut short when the robot's breastplate flipped open. Out came a nasty-looking welding device. The robot's eyes lit up and it barked out a command:

"AUTO-REPAIR ENGAGED."

Danny screamed, and Walter stumbled up the stairs like a bat out of hell. They could hear the robot, still lying on the floor, begin the work of repairing broken wires in its torso.

After they caught their breath, they still had to attend to the matter of Lisa, who was still leaning up against the front door like a board. Grunting and sweating, they dragged their frozen sibling up the stairs.

"You think the door will hold him?" Danny asked as they worked.

"No," Walter replied.

"Great."

"Once he fixes himself, we're screwed," said Walter.

"He's fixing himself?"

"How should I know?"

"You don't have to yell at me," said Danny.

Finally, Lisa was upstairs. Her two brothers hoisted her back into her original position.

"That looks about right," said Walter.

"You think she's okay?"

"I don't want to be around when she wakes up," said Walter. He turned to leave.

"Where're you going?" Danny asked, following him past the piano that still hung stuck in the upper railing, down the stairs, and through the wrecked house.

"I'm taking my turn," said Walter with grim determination.

"You're crazy! That thing's messed up!"

Walter cranked the key and hit the button, and the spinner spun. A six came up, Walter's blue ship moved six spaces, and a new card was spat out of the board. During all this, Danny hid behind the door frame, bracing himself for the worst.

Walter read his card: "'You are promoted to Fleet

Admiral. Go ahead four spaces.'" Danny rolled his eyes as Walter's blue ship thunked ahead another four spaces. "Your turn," said Walter.

"No way."

"Can you just go so I can win this thing and get us home?"

"You're such a jerk," Danny said. He stormed out of the living room.

Walter found him in the kitchen, where he was taking a pot out of the dish drainer. Setting the game on the table, Walter asked, "What are you doing?"

"Making mac and cheese."

"There's no water, dummy. We're in space."

Danny turned on the water and out it came, full force.

"Why are you doing that?" said Walter, not mentioning his mistake.

"Because I'm hungry and I know you're not gonna take care of me," Danny replied.

"Don't bother. The gas won't work."

Danny turned on the front burner. It did work. "Any more advice?" he asked his brother.

"Here. Let me do that," said Walter. "You gotta turn it up more."

Danny turned and stared out the window at the solar system, far, far away.

"Can't we at least talk about this?" said Walter.

"There's nothing to talk about. I'm not going."

"Don't you want to get home?"

"What's so great about home anyway?" Danny said. He was still looking out the window.

"What do you mean?" said Walter. "Everything was great until you came along."

"See what I mean? You treat me like everything's my fault."

"*This* is all your fault. You're the one who pushed the button in the first place."

"I just wanted to play a game with you, Walter."

"I want to go home, Danny, and I can't unless you take your turn."

"That's right. You can't play unless I do too. That means you gotta listen to how I say it is."

"Or else what?" Walter challenged.

"Or else I won't play and we can float out here forever, for all I care."

"I don't believe you."

"Try me," said Danny.

Walter couldn't believe it. Danny had actually called his bluff. "Fine," he said. "What do you want?"

"I want you stop being so mean and ignoring me all the time. I want you to treat me like your brother."

"Fine."

"Do we have an understanding?" Danny said.

"Yeah."

"See? Wasn't that easy?" Danny walked over to the table and smacked the button. The wheel spun. It stopped on a six, and Danny's spaceship clunked ahead six spaces.

When the board spat out a card, Walter took it and read it. "'You are visited by Zorgons.' That's not so bad. Visitors, is all. What's a Zorgon?"

Danny looked over Walter's shoulder in wide-eyed terror. Walter turned to follow Danny's line of vision, toward the dining room. There he saw a stark white searchlight panning through the windows as if looking for them.

Then, outside the kitchen window, a nasty-looking old-fashioned spaceship pulled up right alongside them, keeping pace with the flying house. Bizarre, growly squawks blasted from its speakers, as if some-body was trying to tell them something. The sound was so loud, the windows rattled.

"ZORGONS!" Danny yelled over the din.

"MAYBE THEY'RE FRIENDLY!" Walter yelled back.

Now the barrel of a cannon emerged from a port-hole on the side of the ship and pointed right at them.

"THEY'RE NOT FRIENDLY!" Danny shouted.

Walter scooped up the game board and they took off, running for all they were worth out of the kitchen and toward the living room. "The fireplace! Hide in the fireplace!" Walter yelled.

They dived into the safety of the fireplace, but no sooner had they settled in there than the Zorgon ship banked around the house and pulled up in front of the two broken living room windows. The inside of the laser cannon glowed white-hot, and a ball of searing light fired out, headed straight for the house. The photon blast slammed into the chimney at the top of the house. Walter looked up and saw a cascade of bricks dropping right toward them in the fireplace. "Take cover someplace else!" he screamed.

They both dived out of the chimney just before the bricks crashed to the hearth. Walter ran with the game, and Danny grabbed Richard's cage. They ran into Dad's office, threw themselves to the floor, and covered their heads.

Upstairs, another blast exploded through the wall of Lisa's bedroom. The fiery explosion blew open the bathroom door and then immediately slammed it closed. Frozen Lisa fell over like a sack of potatoes. The entire house shuddered from the blast.

In Dad's office, Danny and Walter uncovered their heads and looked out the window. The Zorgon ship was zipping around them, searching for a new angle of attack. "I told you I didn't want to go! You're the one who made me spin!" Danny hollered.

"There's nothing else we can do!"

The loudspeakers outside kicked in again, the

Zorgons barking unintelligible commands at the house. Danny and Walter cowered under the window ledge, which was the only place they couldn't be seen by the ship. Outside, the laser cannon adjusted its aim and fired another blast at the house. This time it decimated the bottom of the porch and knocked it clean off the front of the house. Walter's bicycle, still floating alongside the house, was blown upward by the force of the blast, tumbling end over end toward the roof.

Walter commando-crawled across the floor and scooped the Zathura game board off the floor, then crawled back and opened it up in front of Danny. He started cranking the key, preparing to take his turn.

"Are you crazy?" Danny said.

"You got any better ideas?"

Walter hit the button and the spinner yielded a six. As Walter's ship moved ahead, the board buzzed and spat out a card. Walter grabbed it. "'Reprogram,'" he read. "What does that mean?"

Well, all he could do was try it. He held the card up in front of him, pointing it toward the windows like an FBI badge. "REPROGRAM!" he ordered.

As if in response, the Zorgon ship leveled another blast at the house. Walter dived out of the way as the missile crashed through the window and slammed into Dad's bookcase, sending reams of artwork cascading through the air.

"It doesn't work!" said Danny, stating the obvious.

Walter shoved the card into his pocket. "We'll figure it out later!" he said. Then he cranked the crank and shoved the game board over to Danny. "Spin!" he said.

"I'm scared!"

"SPIN!" Walter repeated.

Danny smacked the button, the spinner spun a six, and Danny's ship moved ahead. The board spat out a card, which Danny snatched before Walter could get to it.

Behind them, they didn't notice as the Zorgon ship moved past, revealing a white speck that was visible in the distance outside the window—a white speck that was growing larger.

"What's it say?" Walter wanted to know.

Danny squinted at the card. "'Rest on standing AstroTurf'!" he said.

"Huh?"

The white speck, unseen by either of them, was larger still. Now it was recognizable as a human form, and it was tumbling straight for their window.

Danny was still trying to figure out the card. "'Rest on standing AstroTurf'? I don't get it!"

Walter reached for the card. "Oh, let me!" he said.

Danny held the card away from him. "I know how to read!" he said.

Danny squirmed away, but Walter grabbed him and pinned his hand to the floor. With great effort,

Danny found an old game in the basement.

At each turn a card would pop out of the side of the game.

The first card started a meteor shower that blew holes in the roof!

Lisa was frozen in a cryonic sleep.

A defective robot was bent on destroying Walter.

The powerful gravity of Tsouris-3 almost pulled Danny into space.

The astronaut used his jetpack to bring Walter to safety.

The boys tried to finish the game so they could return home.

Danny had to be lowered in the dumbwaiter to get the game back.

Danny and Walter had to play the game until they reached Zathura.

"What's a pilot light?" Walter asked.

"In the basement," said the astronaut over his shoulder. "Little blue flame under the big heater. Just blow it out like a candle." He lifted the top of the stove and chucked it to the side. Then he bent to blow out the stove's pilot light. "Like this," he said, blowing out the blue flame.

Danny, in the meantime, ran into the living room. He put the gerbil cage on the floor and hit the lights. Then he ran upstairs and through the hallway, turning out the lights one by one.

The astronaut hurried into the living room and began searching around in the rubble, looking for something in particular. Aha—there it was. His eyes lit up as he spied a small wooden box of fireplace matches. He flicked it open.

Walter walked nervously down the stairs toward the basement door as another photon blast hit the house hard. But as he reached for the doorknob, he noticed something in the crack under the door.

Sparks. Like from a welding torch.

He leaned closer to the door and laid his ear against it. Inside, he could hear machinery: a little saw, a power screwdriver . . . and the robot's muffled voice, giving itself repair instructions.

He turned and raced back upstairs without opening the door.

Well, he definitely couldn't blow out the pilot light



he pried Danny's fingers open and read the card.

"'Rescue stranded astronaut'!" he read.

"What stranded astronaut?" Danny asked.

*BOOM BOOM BOOM!*

They whirled and finally saw what had been heading their way. It was an astronaut in a space suit. He slammed into the window. Upside down.

Walter was startled. He couldn't see the astronaut's face through the reflective visor on his helmet. He just saw a big distorted image of himself.

The Zorgon ship had still not given up. It blasted past them from behind the astronaut, sending him cartwheeling away from the window, swept along in the ship's wake.

For a moment, all was silent. The boys looked at each other. Maybe he'd gone away?

*DING-DONG.*

He hadn't gone away. He was ringing the doorbell. The doorknob was turning!

They drew in their breath . . .

"Did you lock the door?" said Danny.

"Who locks their door in outer space?" Walter said.

A second later, the front door banged open, slamming up against the wall to reveal the astronaut in full glory. He was still upside down, however.

A square pack was strapped to his back. It was a propulsion system that he could operate by squeezing the right and left handles on which he rested his hands. This gave him little bursts of power that controlled his speed and direction. He squeezed a handle and his propulsion pack made a hissing noise on one side, rotating him counterclockwise to an upright position.

Now he squeezed both handles and shot forward, floating into the center of the entry hall and thudding down on his boots as the house's gravity took hold of him. He pushed the door shut behind him and turned toward the boys.

They cowered in the corner, having no idea what to make of this guy. Danny clutched his gerbil cage. The astronaut took off his helmet, revealing a scruffy-looking man. He loomed over the two kids, who were too stunned to run.

"Which one of you spun me?" he said.

*KA-BOOM!* Another Zorgon blast shook the house to its foundations. The boys jumped, startled by the blast, but the astronaut stood tall and strong. "Who was it?" he repeated.

Wide-eyed, Walter pointed to Danny. "He did."

The astronaut leaned in to Walter and spoke very firmly. "Don't be so quick to sell out your brother, kid," he said. "He's all you got."

*Zorrch!* A photon blast cut through the house behind the astronaut and exploded, sending debris into the room. Again, the stranger didn't flinch.



"Looks like you have a serious Zorgon problem to deal with," he said.

"What do we do?" Walter asked him. He was willing to take help from anybody.

"Hide," said the astronaut.

"Hide?" said Danny. "They'll just explode the whole house!"

The astronaut looked at Danny. Just the sight of the little kid seemed to charm him. "We're going to hide the house," he explained.

They moved to the kitchen. Danny and Walter crouched on the kitchen floor behind the astronaut, who began rummaging through the cabinet under the sink and throwing junk into the room. "Go turn off all the lights and electrical appliances," he said, talking fast as the rumbling Zorgon ship circled outside the windows.

"Me?" said Danny.

"Do it!" barked the astronaut.

Danny ran off to follow orders, and the astronaut turned to Walter. "You, kill that flame on the stove."

Walter turned and saw the still lit burner on the stove.

Now the stranger found what he was looking for—a can of lighter fluid. "Burning gas," he muttered, "that's probably what brought 'em in the first place." He turned to Walter again. "And then hit the pilot light on the furnace," he said.

with the robot in the way. But Walter had another idea. He ran up the back stairs to the second floor and sprinted down the hallway to a gadget on the wall at the far end: the thermostat. Giving himself a little smile for his ingenuity, he quickly turned it down, way down, below fifty.

In the basement, the bright yellow flame under the furnace guttered out. But the blue pilot light burned on, almost as bright as the sparks from the robot on the floor.

Upstairs, Danny ran over to Walter, all out of breath. "The astronaut guy's wrecking Dad's couch!" he said, shocked. They ran down to the foyer to discover that the astronaut was, indeed, wrecking Dad's couch. He was dousing it with the flammable lighter fluid.

"That's Dad's nap couch!" Walter told him.

But the astronaut, without blinking an eye, tossed a match at the couch, and the fabric instantly burst into flame. "Open the front door!" he ordered Danny. "Give me a shoulder here!" he said to Walter.

Danny ran to the door and flung it open as the astronaut hunkered down behind the couch, rammed his shoulder against the part of it that had not yet caught on fire, and pushed hard. Walter joined in, and together they shoved the thing all the way across the foyer and out the front door. Blazing, the sofa sailed off into the great black void.

Danny, Walter, and the astronaut stood in the open doorway, watching as the burning couch drifted off. "Go on," the astronaut said under his breath, "follow . . . follow . . ."

"What's happening?" Walter asked him.

The astronaut was still watching the sofa's flight intently. "Zorgons are like lizards," he explained, "cold-blooded, so they're heat seekers. Even the tiniest spark of warmth draws them like moths. They fly all over the galaxy looking for things to burn up."

"Why don't they go burn up their own planet?" Walter grumbled.

"Already did," said the astronaut. "But that's not the worst part. The real problem is their appetites. They never stop eating."

"Wh-what do they eat?" Walter asked, afraid to find out.

"Meat," said the astronaut.

"Well, that's good," said Danny, relieved.

"Dude—you're meat," said the astronaut.

Danny gasped.

Through the open front door, they saw the Zorgon ship heel over to starboard and turn to follow the flaming couch. They watched as it disappeared into the vast reaches of space. The astronaut sighed in relief. "You have no idea how close that was," he said.

Back in the darkened kitchen, the astronaut opened the door to the refrigerator and shined his flashlight inside. He reached in and started pulling out packages of meat, slapped them down on the kitchen table, and began opening them all.

Walter appeared in the kitchen doorway. "What are you doing?" he asked.

"Are you doing this to keep Zorgons away?" Danny said.

The astronaut found a bag of white bread and dumped the contents onto the counter. "I'm doing this," he said, "because I haven't had food you can chew in twelve years."

The astronaut ate like a prisoner, one arm guarding his vittles. He was now stripped down to a T-shirt. The two boys watched from the doorway, afraid to approach.

"This totally sucks," said Walter quietly to his brother.

"Why?" said Danny.

"He's eating all our food."

"So? Lupe just went shopping," said Danny.

"So? How do you know how long we'll be drifting out here? It could be weeks. Or even years. Then what?"

"I don't know," Danny replied.

"And what about our air?" Walter went on. "How long you think that will last with him breathing it all?"

"I guess," mumbled Danny.

"I'm gonna say something," said Walter. He approached the chewing space man as Danny watched from a safe distance. "Dude. That's our food," he said.

"Yeah. By the way, you're running low on supplies," said the astronaut, his mouth full.

"Yeah. I know. You're eating it all."

"Oh, I'm sorry. Am I eating too much of your *food?*" said the astronaut, his voice dripping with sarcasm.

"It's just, we might be out here for a while."

"Oh, really? You know how long I've been out here? Twelve *years.*"

"That sucks, bro, but that's our food," said Walter.

"If I'm not mistaken, the card said 'Rescue stranded astronaut.' Looks to me like I'm the one who rescued the two of you. The least you can do is pay me the common courtesy of a few bites of food."

"Homey, you're eating it all," said Walter, not giving ground.

"I traveled through a time sphincter to get here.

Do you have any idea how difficult that is?"

"What's a time sphincter?" Danny asked.

"It's a wormhole, about yay big," said the astronaut, making a circle with his thumb and forefinger. "Squeeze through one of those and tell me you're not hungry enough to eat a carpet shark."

"Sounds like you got a big trip home ahead of you," said Walter coldly.

"You telling me to leave?" said the astronaut.

"When you're done eating. Yeah."

The astronaut jerked a thumb toward Danny. "With all due respect, he spun me. It's up to him," he told Walter.

"Well, I happen to be a Fleet Admiral," said Walter, "and I'm telling you to go."

"Really?" said the astronaut, looking shocked.

Walter showed him his admiral card. "Yeah. See?"

"I apologize, sir," said the astronaut. "I had no idea. Wait a minute . . ." He theatrically reached into his T-shirt pocket for his own card. "I'm a Fleet Admiral too, bugnuts. It's just a card."

Walter was deflated but not defeated. "Well, *he* wants you to leave too," he said, pointing his chin toward Danny.

"That true, Danny?" said the astronaut. "You want me to go?"

"Of course he does," said Walter.

"I gotta hear it from the big guy," said the astronaut.

"Well . . . " said Danny.

"Danny. Tell him to leave," Walter said.

Danny wasn't so sure. "He did help . . ."

"I'll tell you what he did," said Walter. "He burnt our furniture and ate all our food."

"Yeah," said the astronaut, "you guys were doing an incredible job before I got here. The place looks great. You clearly had everything covered just fine."

"He helped with the Zorgons. Good," Walter said to Danny. "They're gone."

"For now," said the astronaut.

"Whatever. We're almost done. A few more rolls and we're home."

"I've been part of this game for twelve years. I might know a thing or two."

"Maybe he can help," Danny said in a small voice.

"Whose brother are you? His or mine?" Walter demanded.

Danny was quiet for a long time, thinking. "He stays," he said finally.

Walter made a face. How could Danny make such a dumb call?

The astronaut picked up his sandwich and carried it with him toward the living room. "Come on," he called back to Walter. "It's your turn. 'Admiral.'"

In the ruined living room, Walter, Danny, and the astronaut sat down around the board. Danny and the astronaut were on the living room side of the board.

Walter, on the other side, was actually sitting in the foyer.

"All right," said the astronaut, rallying the boys. "Let's see. Got the key?"

"Wait a minute," said Walter. "Something's wrong."

"What?" said the astronaut.

"I was ahead of you," Walter told Danny.

"Somebody must've kicked the board," said Danny.

"Nobody kicked the board!" Walter yelled. "The pieces are attached! He cheated!"

"No, I didn't!"

"I knew it! I knew you'd cheat!"

"Easy, guys, easy," said the astronaut. "Did you move the piece?" he asked Danny.

"Maybe I moved it by accident," Danny said.

"I knew it!" said Walter.

"Take it easy," the astronaut said to him. "Where were you?" he asked Danny.

"There," said Danny, pointing.

"He was on the blue circle," said Walter.

"Oh, right," Danny said, remembering.

Walter pointed to a space on the board. "I was here." He gave the piece a hard tug and it made a sound that suggested that the game wasn't designed to do such things. They all winced.

Nothing bad happened.

"Everybody happy now?" the astronaut asked. "All better?"

Walter shook his head at Danny. "What a baby," he said.

"I'm not a baby."

Walter slapped the button and the spinner spun, but it kept spinning. It didn't stop. "Great," he said to his brother. "You broke it."

The board buzzed and spat out a yellow card, which Walter snatched from the board and read: "'Caught cheating. Automatic ejection.'"

The three of them looked at each other, confused. The game had stopped buzzing.

"Do you think it means me?" Walter said. "Danny was the one who cheated. I was just putting it—" In a fraction of a second, Walter was launched like a missile into the air and out the asteroid hole in the roof.

Danny and the astronaut looked up and saw that Walter had managed to grab hold of a beam sticking out of the jagged edge of the hole in the roof, which saved him from sailing out into the blackness. Unfortunately, that still left him dangling upside down over the house as it moved through outer space. He was screaming at the top of his lungs.

The astronaut turned and, for some reason, left the room.

"Hang on, Walter, I'll save you!" Danny yelled. He raced up the stairs onto the second-floor landing and ran over to stand beneath the hole. "Hang on!" he said again.

"Throw me something and pull me down!" Walter called.

"Right!" Danny looked around for something he could use, but he couldn't see anything. "Like what?" he called up to Walter.

"Something with a cord on it!"

"Right!"

Danny spotted a lamp on a hallway table. The outlet was some distance away and the lamp was plugged in to an extension cord, so there was a good ten feet of length. He unplugged it. "Catch!" he said, throwing the lamp to Danny.

It whacked Walter in the head and flew past him. "Oww!" he yelped.

As it shot past him, Walter grabbed the cord. The other end of the cord flew past as well. Danny hadn't held on to the other end. Useless. Walter let go. "Danny, throw me something with a cord on it AND HOLD ON TO THE OTHER END, YOU IDIOT!" he yelled.

"Sorry!"

Now Danny heard the astronaut's voice behind him. "Stand back, Danny!" he said. Danny turned around and there was the astronaut, wearing his jetpack. He rocketed up to the hole in the ceiling and grabbed Walter. The two of them plummeted downward and landed hard on the wooden floor below.

Danny ran down the stairs and tried to help Walter

get up. "Get away from me," Walter snapped at him.

"I'm sorry," Danny quavered.

"Don't talk to me until we get home," said Walter.

"I said I was sorry—"

Walter left Danny in midsentence and went downstairs to the living room, where the astronaut had gone back to the game board.

"Everybody okay?" said the astronaut, trying to lighten things up. "See? Not such a big deal. Little speed bump is all."

"Why the heck did it punish me?" Walter grumbled. "He's the one who cheated."

"It's like a pinball machine. If you tamper with it, it tilts," said the astronaut.

"Let's just play so I can get away from him," said Walter.

"I told him I was sorry," Danny said.

"Let's all get our heads right and pull it together. You're up, big man," the astronaut told Danny. "Don't worry. I got ya."

Danny sat down, cranked the key, and hit the spin button. He got an eight. His rocket ship rattled forward and stopped on a new space, whereupon the board buzzed and Danny grabbed his card. He was trying to read it, moving his lips silently.

"What's it say?" asked the astronaut.

"He can't read," said Walter with contempt. Then he snatched the card out of Danny's hand and read it:

Walter didn't notice. "Cool. Hey, I'm almost to the end. Only a few more and I win!"

The board buzzed out Walter's card. This one was gold. "'Shooting star. Make a wish as it passes,'" he read. He looked up at the others, thrilled. "That's gotta be the best card in the whole game!"

"Just make your stupid wish, already!" Danny said. "I just want to go home! I don't even care who wins!"

"That's 'cause you never win at anything!" Walter said.

"Walter . . ." said the astronaut.

"No!" Walter kept on, ignoring him. "That's why he cheats all the time!"

"No, I don't!" said Danny.

"Guys, guys—"

Walter continued to ignore the astronaut. "Yes, you do! You almost got me killed!" he yelled at Danny.

"I don't care if I did!"

"OH, YEAH? IT'S YOUR FAULT MOM AND DAD GOT DIVORCED!" Walter bellowed.

Danny couldn't believe his ears. That one was way below the belt.

"Walter!" said the astronaut, shocked.

Danny picked up the game and hurled it at Walter, who ducked out of the way. The game smashed against the wall in the corner of the living room. It smacked off the plaster, banged into the other wall, and dropped to the floor upside down. "You suck!"

Danny yelled, close to tears. He turned, stormed out of the room, and raced upstairs. They heard his feet booming down the hall, and then the door of the bedroom slammed in the distance.

Walter was unfazed. Outside, he could see a very bright light, and it was hurtling toward them. The shooting star. "I get my wish now, don't I?" he asked the astronaut.

"The moment it passes, yeah." The astronaut did not look excited.

The living room was now bathed in a brilliant light. Walter and the astronaut turned and squinted out the big picture window. The huge, glowing fireball was closing in fast.

"Don't do it, Walter," said the astronaut.

"Don't do what?"

"Don't wish what you're thinking."

The star came closer.

"You don't know what I'm thinking," Walter said.

"I can tell it isn't good."

Drawn to the window, Walter stared outside, an idea forming in his mind that was every bit as dark as the star was bright. The shooting star was just ten seconds away now.

"I'm telling you," said the astronaut, "no matter how good an idea seems when you're mad—"

A shadow passed over Walter's face. He was thinking something awful, but he still wouldn't look at the astronaut. They could the hear the shooting star now, a hot sizzling *whoosh* that grew louder and louder. Five seconds away.

"—it isn't. You gotta believe me on this one," the astronaut finished.

With a crackling roar, the star passed just outside the living room windows, its dazzling light washing the whole room hot white for one spectacular moment as Walter squinted his eyes, making his wish.

And then it was gone.

As the room returned to normal, it was as if Walter had come out from under a spell. He shook his head to clear it and turned away from the window.

"What did you wish?" said the astronaut.

"I can't tell you."

*"What did you wish?"*

"You know the rules about wishes," Walter said stubbornly. "It won't come true."

The astronaut grabbed him by the arms and spun him around. "Tell me!" he shouted. "Tell me!"

Walter stared at him. "What's the matter with you?"

The astronaut let him go. He turned and looked upstairs. "You did it, didn't you?" he said.

He took off for the stairs, bounding up them three at a time. "Danny?" he yelled. When he reached the top, he raced down the hallway. *"Danny?"*

There was no answer from the other end of the

hall. He reached the door to the boys' room and threw it open, looking everyplace at once. There was no one in the room. He stepped inside the room and cast his eyes around it. Nobody. His shoulders sagged. "Oh, no," he whispered bleakly.

Walter walked into the room holding a football. Immediately, the astronaut was on him, grabbing him and shaking him by the shoulders.

"What?" said Walter, confused and frightened.

*"How could you do that to him?"*

"Do what?"

"Don't play with me! I got a read on you like you wouldn't believe!"

"Take it easy," said Walter, getting a little freaked out.

"You have no idea the life of misery you've brought upon yourself," said the astronaut.

"Because of a football?"

"Leave him alone!" said Danny's voice. The astronaut turned to see Danny scrambling out from under his bed in his brother's defense.

The astronaut was visibly confused as he released Walter. "What did you wish for?" he said, trying to get his composure back.

Walter was still shaken as he held out the football.

"You wished for a football?" the astronaut said.

"It's autographed by Brett Favre," said Walter.

Danny could not believe it. "You coulda wished us

home! You coulda wished the game over!" he yelled at Walter.

"Well, I was under a lot of pressure." He pointed to the astronaut. "He was yelling at me."

"It doesn't work that way," said the astronaut. "Trust me. Once you start the game, you gotta finish it."

"You're acting really weird," said Danny. "I think I want you to leave now."

They kept an eye on him as he collected himself and sat down on Walter's bed. "Twelve years ago," he said, "I sat down to play this very same game with my brother."

"You're a player?" said Walter.

"Yeah. Just like you. And me and my brother, we were fighting a lot back then, and when the game started things got even worse."

"Just like us," said Danny.

"Yeah. As the game went on I got madder and madder. And I landed on the star space, the same one Walter just landed on. And . . . you know how you get sometimes, it's like you're not in charge of what you're thinking in your own head?"

"Yeah," said Walter.

"I was so mad," said the astronaut, "that when that star passed, I made my wish. And my wish was . . . I wished my brother had never been born. But as soon as I did it, I felt horrible. I tried to spin again—I thought maybe I could land on another star and wish him back, but the game wouldn't let me go, because it wasn't my turn." He looked right at Walter. "There are some games you can't play alone," he said.

He wiped some sweat from his forehead and continued. "And I've been wandering around the universe inside this stupid game ever since, looking for a way to get my brother back, and get us both out of here."

"So what do we do now?" said Walter.

"We go downstairs," said the astronaut, "and we finish this thing, once and for all. No more cheating, no more arguing: all you guys have to do is spin the wheel a few times. I'll help you fight off whatever comes out, and then maybe, maybe if you guys finish it, you can go home. Deal?"

"Deal," said Danny.

The astronaut's face was looking sort of red. "Is it getting warm in here?" he said. They looked at each other and the astronaut reached up and wiped his forehead. He came away with a palm full of sweat.

He looked at Walter, concern creasing his brow. "You blew out the pilot light on the furnace, right?"

"Um . . ."

There was a great and horrible wrenching sound from downstairs, the sound of wood splintering, metal shrieking, and glass shattering. The astronaut jumped to his feet and signaled for the kids to hush. "Stay put," he whispered. He tiptoed out the door, and the boys could hear him stealthily making his way down the stairs.

Naturally ignoring his advice, the boys peeked over the second-floor railing. They watched him pause at the foot of the stairs, disturbed by whatever it was that he was seeing down there. The kids followed him down.

"Zorgons," the astronaut hissed.

When Danny and Walter got downstairs, they could see what the problem was. The front corner of the house had been torn off.

The living room looked as if a huge shark had swum by and taken a bite out of it. The whole front corner was opened up to outer space.

"My gerbil was in there," said Danny.

"This is bad. This is very bad," the astronaut said.

"Why?" said Walter. "We didn't get eaten."

"They found us again," said the astronaut.

Walter was still not worried. "So? They got what they wanted."

"No," the astronaut replied, "they got a taste. When that ship gets back to the swarm it's gonna tell all its buddies where we are, and they'll crack this house open like a lobster and pick it clean."

Now Walter got it.

The boys peered fearfully out into space. It was easy to get a good view. They just had to look through the jagged maw that had been the corner of their living room.

"So what do we do?" Danny asked.

"We finish the game and get you guys home," said the astronaut.

"Right!" said Walter, snapping to it. "Where's the game?"

"In the living room," said Danny.

There was a sudden dead silence. As one, the three of them turned and looked out into space through the missing chunk of house.

"Uh-oh?" Danny guessed.

"They ate it?" tried Walter.

"Burned. They'll want to burn it," said the astronaut.

Danny and Walter stared in shock and dismay. Now what would they do?

"We're dead," said Walter.

"We're not dead," said the astronaut.

Walter was really panicking now. "Oh, no?" he said. "We're floating out here like a ham in a piranha tank!"

"Stop it. You're scaring me," said Danny.

"We'll figure something out," said the astronaut, trying to calm them down.

"What are you talking about?" said Walter. "We can't get back without the game, the Zorgons have the game, and they're gone! We'll never be able to find them."

"Then they'll just have to find us," said the astronaut grimly.

They followed him to the kitchen, where he immediately began working on his plan. It started with swinging a kitchen chair down onto the edge of the counter as hard as he could, smashing it to bits. Then he picked up another one and smashed that one to bits too. He did the same with a third, tossing the pieces onto a pile he was making in the big fireplace in the kitchen.

Next he sent them on a trip to Dad's office. *Crash!* Grunting, Danny and Walter tipped over the big bookcase in Dad's office. An ocean of paper spilled out onto the floor. They scooped up as much as they could carry, headed into the kitchen, and hurled it into the fireplace, where the astronaut had lit a fire. It had started out small but by now it was not a bad little blaze. The astronaut stepped back and looked at it. "More," he ordered.

So they got more. Stuff started flying into the jammed-up fireplace: pillows, boxes of cereal, anything remotely combustible.

The three of them stepped back and looked at the fire. It was really getting there; the flames were licking out of the fireplace and up the wall.

"More!" said the astronaut.

Up in her bathroom, Lisa, fully thawed now, was blow-drying her hair. She stopped and sniffed the air, turned off the blow dryer, and sniffed again. She definitely smelled something. What were those little pains up to? She opened the door to her bedroom.

Her bed was standing on its headboard, and her stuff was strewn all over the floor. She was looking at the effects of Tsouris-3, but of course, not knowing that, she blamed her brothers. "I'm gonna kill them," she muttered.

Leaving the bathroom, she ran down the stairs and toward the kitchen, where she found black smoke pouring from underneath the swinging door. "OH MY GOD!" she shrieked. She ran toward the door, pushed it open, and instantly recoiled from the intense heat of the bonfire inside.

"OH MY GOD!" she shrieked again, just in time to see Walter and Danny throw a pile of dirty laundry into the fireplace, which had no more room for anything now and was spitting out six-foot tongues of flame that reached the ceiling. "YOU SET THE HOUSE ON FIRE! YOU REALLY SET THE HOUSE ON FIRE!" she screamed.

They turned and saw her, broke into huge, relieved smiles, and ran to hug her.

"You're okay!" yelled Walter.

"Lisa's back!" yelled Danny at the same time.

"Get off me!" she snarled at them. "Where's the fire extinguisher?" She started ripping through the cabinets, searching for it. Finding it, she pointed the nozzle at the fireplace and pulled the handle. An enormous *sploosh* of foam shot out and blanketed the fire.

Walter and Danny started yelling at once. "Nooo! Stop! We need to attract the Zorgons!" But Lisa kept blasting until the fireplace was full of foam.

"Great," said Walter.

"Don't worry," said the astronaut, who was standing in the opposite door of the kitchen. "It worked."

Lisa, who had not noticed him before, jumped about a foot. "WHO ARE YOU?" she yelled.

But he was already heading for the living room, so they followed him. The bright searchlight of a Zorgon ship bathed the ruins of the living room as the vessel closed in broadside.

Lisa stared out the hole in the house. For the first time, she realized that they were in outer space. "Ahhhhhhh!" she screamed.

"Stop screaming!" Walter said to her. "We're trying to be proactive."

"They're going to board us," said the astronaut. "We gotta somehow—"

"WHO'S BOARDING US?" Lisa cut in. "WILL SOMEBODY PLEASE TALK TO ME?"

"The Zorgons," said Walter.

"What are Zorgons?"

"They're lizard men," said Danny. "They eat meat." He paused. "*We're* meat," he added.

*Wham!* The house rocked as two enormous harpoons crunched through the walls and splayed open, anchoring themselves. The first Zorgon ship reeled them in, pulling itself closer, toward the bottom of the house.

Lisa ran off in a panic. "We gotta hide! Downstairs! Follow me!" she yelled. She raced out of the room, expecting the others to follow, but they paid no attention whatever to her.

"Once they dock," said the astronaut, "I'll look for the game on their ship."

*"You're going onto their ship?"* said Danny.

"You want to go home?" said the astronaut.

"More than anything," said Danny.

Walter wasn't listening to this conversation. He was having a thought. "Did she say 'downstairs'?" he said.

Lisa had definitely said "downstairs." "Come on, you guys!" she called urgently, starting down herself. "We'll be safe in here—hurry!" She threw open the bottom basement door.

There, at the foot of the stairs, was the half-repaired robot sitting up and drilling its own head. "ALIEN LIFE FORM. MUST DES—" it was saying.

Lisa screamed, slammed the door shut in the robot's face, and raced back up the stairs.

In the kitchen she met the astronaut, Walter, and Danny, who were just turning the corner to find her. "Just stay with us and everything will be okay," said the astronaut.

"I'll never leave you," blubbered Lisa, by now a total mess.

Behind them, the Zorgon ships were visible outside through the ripped-off corner of the living room.

"We gotta hide!" said the astronaut.

They ran up the stairs to the second floor as a Zorgon ship crunched into the living room, towed in by the harpoon cables. Studs and joists snapped like Popsicle sticks as the metal hulk sucked up against the house.

Two more harpoons hit on either side of the asteroid hole in the roof. One penetrated the second-floor hallway landing. As the chain pulled taut, the entire landing was ripped out.

All four of them ran toward the laundry room and crammed inside, huddling on the floor in front of the washer and dryer with the lights out. The astronaut had grabbed Walter's set of walkie-talkies and was working on the broken antenna.

"You guys wait here," he said. "I'll keep in touch with these."

"They're not gonna work," said Walter. "Danny broke 'em—they're completely destroyed. He—"

The astronaut easily snapped the "broken" antenna back into place.

"Oh," said Walter sheepishly.

The astronaut handed the walkie-talkie to Walter. "Keep the volume low," he said. "Use this only if you need me."

"Where are you gonna be?" asked Danny.

"I'm going to get the game back," said the astronaut. He slipped out the door and closed it behind him, leaving the three kids alone. The only light they had came from the crack beneath the door.

Lisa stared after the astronaut, fascinated. "Wow," she said. "That guy—who is he? I just feel so . . . so safe around him."

"Oh, brother," said Walter.

"What? He obviously feels very protective of me . . . if we get out of this, who knows?" She looked dreamy. "He has gorgeous eyes," she added.

The walkie-talkie hissed to life, and the astronaut's voice came in. "Zorgons," he said in hushed tones.

The kids huddled around the thing, listening breathlessly. "Oh, God," he whispered, "the place is crawling with them." Static was making his voice cut in and out. ". . . basement . . . corner . . . see the game! Box is right there! Hang on, I'll get closer!"

There was bumping and rustling on the other end.

"Did he get the game?" Danny asked.

Now the astronaut's voice again, sounding panicky: "I . . . no . . . Th . . . No, no, don't, I—" There was a frantic rustling for a few seconds, and then the transmission abruptly cut out.

Walter was desperate. "Hello?" he yelled into the unit. "Are you there? Hello?"

Silence. They looked at one another, terrified. Finally, Danny said what was on their minds. "Is he . . . dead?"

They heard heavy footsteps, and the shadow of a

figure appeared in the crack under the door. They held their breath.

*Wham!* The closet door jerked open. They were all about to scream when they realized it was the astronaut, who had returned. He closed the door quickly behind him and hunched down in front of them, speaking in an urgent whisper.

"The game was right there," he said, "right underneath a little box with sliding doors on the front, but I couldn't get to it! There's too many of them. All over the basement."

"Are there any upstairs?" Walter asked.

"Not yet. But, once they're done down there . . ." He took a moment, catching his breath.

Lisa reached over and put her hand on his. "You did your best," she said, moving a little closer to him. "We believe in you."

"Will you please!" Walter said in disgust.

Suddenly Danny spoke out of the blue. "The dumbwaiter," he said.

"What?" said the astronaut.

"The sliding-doors thing you saw," Danny told him. "It's that little elevator. You could sneak down from upstairs in it. Couldn't he, Walter?"

"Yeah," said Walter.

"All you'd have to do," Danny went on, "is reach out and grab the game and we'll pull you back up! It's easy!"

"But he's too big," Walter said.

"You're right," Danny agreed. "Too bad. It was a good idea."

"It was a great idea," said the astronaut.

"Yeah," Lisa said.

"It was," said Walter.

"Too bad he won't fit," said Danny. He trailed off as he noticed that they were all staring at him. "Do we really need the game?" he said in a tiny voice.

About two minutes later, Danny was jammed into the dumbwaiter box on the second-floor landing, his knees crunched up against his chest. Even he barely fit; nobody else would have stood a chance.

Lisa and the astronaut kept an eye on both stairwells as Walter checked in with his frightened brother. They each tried to put on a face of courage for the other's sake.

"How you doing?" Walter asked.

"Okay, I guess," said Danny.

"Listen to me," said Walter. "All you gotta do is ride down in this thing and grab the game, and we'll pull you right up."

"Right."

"Nothing's gonna happen to you."

"Yeah."

"'Cause I'm your brother. And that's what being a brother means. It means I'll never let anything happen to you."

"Yeah."

"You understand?" said Walter. He looked right into Danny's eyes.

"Yeah."

"Okay," said Walter. "This'll only take a few seconds." He turned to leave, but Danny stopped him.

"Hey, Walter?" Danny said.

"Yeah?"

"I'm sorry I cheated."

"That's okay," said Walter.

The astronaut returned and handed Danny a walkie-talkie. "Coast is clear," he said. "Ready to do this?"

"Let's roll," said Danny.

The astronaut reached for the rope. He started to pull it, hand over hand, and the box began to move. Danny sank out of view as Walter watched.

Inside the dark chute, Danny-in-a-box kept going down, down, down, hugging his knees and looking miserable. The chute seemed to go down forever, toward a blazing bright spot at the bottom.

Unseen by any of them, the pulley that supported the whole apparatus was still straining at its screws. Now it started to warp and splinter.

The astronaut continued pulling, hand over hand. Walter watched the back stairs, Lisa the front.

In the box, Danny passed the first floor. Halfway there . . .

Up on the landing, Walter joined the astronaut,

helping to lower Danny. Suddenly Lisa whispered: "Stop! Get down!"

The astronaut and Walter froze and stopped lowering Danny. They crouched down low, the astronaut still holding the rope.

"Don't move!" Lisa hissed.

They followed her gaze to a Zorgon shadow on the wall above them. It turned, looking in all directions.

Danny could feel that he had stopped, but he was not yet at the bottom. He wriggled, trying to move again. "Hey. Why'd you stop?" he said into the walkie-talkie. He twisted around, trying to look up at them. "Come on!" Trying to get the box moving, he rocked back and forth.

With a loud splintering sound, the screws came free.

The pulley yanked out of the ceiling and the rope started whizzing through the astronaut's hands, and Danny cried out as the box went into free fall.

All the noise attracted the Zorgon's attention. The shadow on the wall turned abruptly toward them.

"Help me!" the astronaut whispered, his hands on fire as he tried to hang on to the rope. Walter lunged over and grabbed hold, and together they stopped the rope and held it fast. The box containing Danny jerked to a sudden stop, right above the basement floor.

Danny's heart was in his mouth. He peered out through the crack in the dumbwaiter's door, but he couldn't see much. The sounds coming from the other side, though, were certainly scary—the throb of a motor, the roar of a hungry inferno, the growls of Zorgons.

Summoning all his courage, Danny took a deep breath and slowly slid open the creaky door. He looked around the basement. It had been a creepy place before, but now it was a hundred times worse, lit by the uneven orange light of a fire. An entire section of the cellar was missing below the living room. A Zorgon furnace ship was backed up to the cellar, white-hot flames raging within it. Danny put the walkie-talkie in his pocket and got ready to climb out of the dumbwaiter.

Danny looked down. Below him on the floor, just barely at arm's reach, was the Zathura game box. He leaned out as far as he dared; he could almost touch it.

Upstairs, as Walter and the astronaut strained to hold the dumbwaiter rope, the shadow of the Zorgon on the wall behind them started getting larger. It was getting closer. A disgusting Zorgon snout appeared and a slimy tongue sniffed the air.

"It's coming up the stairs!" whispered Lisa, hardly breathing.

In the basement, Danny opened the dumbwaiter door all the way and crawled out of it as slowly and quietly as possible. As soon as he was down on the ground he snatched the box.

But it was too light. It was only the top of the box. It was not the game.

He crouched down and took a look around the basement. All was clear. The basement was stacked to the ceiling with piles of debris that the Zorgons had stripped from the house. They were using it as a staging area.

Just inside the doors of the Zorgon ship, there was another giant pile of stolen, burnable junk. The firelight coming from inside the ship glinted off something metallic.

It was the game!

Despite the fact that every ounce of him wanted to run the other way, Danny crept across the basement toward it. He was almost there when he heard a growling from his right, inside the basement. He ducked his head and turned.

In the corner, a group of Zorgons were crowded together. They were barking and snapping, fighting over whatever it was they were gathered around.

Then something flew out from the middle of the group and skittered across the basement floor, coming to a stop at Danny's feet. It was the gerbil's empty cage. The water bottle was still dripping.

Danny steeled himself. He would not cry. He had a job to do.

Elsewhere in the house, a Zorgon was climbing slowly up the stairs to the second floor. Lisa saw it. She crawled over to the astronaut. “It’s coming!” she whispered.

“Get out of here, both of you! Hide!” said the astronaut.

Walter and Lisa ran down the hall. The astronaut, who was still holding the rope, looked around. What the heck was he going do with it?

Danny, meanwhile, had reached the torn edge of the basement and was now at the entrance to the Zorgon ship. He gingerly hopped across a small gap between the house and the ship, with only black space below it. From here he could see that the pile of junk was being shoveled onto a conveyor belt, which led to the open mouth of a blast furnace in the bowels of the Zorgon ship.

Suddenly, a shovel crunched into the pile not three feet from where Danny was hiding. His eyes opened wide as his gaze followed the shovel handle up to whoever was holding it.

Or whatever was holding it. Definitely whatever: it was a Zorgon, hideously green and scaly, with a ruby-handled broadsword dangling at its side. The creature looked much, much worse than Danny had imagined.

As the Zorgon turned with the shovelful of junk, Danny looked up at the top of the pile. The Zathura game board was there, just out of reach, way on top. It was charred and scarred, but basically intact.

Danny reached up as high as his arm would

stretch, trying to grab the board. He was able to tap it with his fingers, and it began to teeter off the pile. Suddenly, the walkie-talkie in his pocket went off. The Zorgon heard the sound.

"They're coming," said the astronaut's crackly voice over the unit. "Where are you?" Danny rifled frantically through his pockets, looking for the radio as the Zorgon followed the sound around the pile of junk.

Oh, no. Danny watched helplessly as the game fell onto the conveyor belt and started moving inexorably toward the blast furnace.

"They're up here," said the astronaut's voice. "We saw one."

Now the Zorgon was really irked. Rummaging around the trash pile for the noise, it finally found the crackling walkie-talkie. But Danny was gone. All that was left was the squawking box left sitting on the floor. The Zorgon squealed and smashed it with his shovel.

Danny had to get that game. He sprinted alongside the conveyor belt, keeping his head low, following the Zathura board.

Up on the second floor, things were not going much better. The Zorgon had now gotten all the way up to the second-floor landing. But there was nobody up there. There was, however, a rope, conspicuously tied to the railing, leading down into the dumbwaiter chute.

The Zorgon stepped forward to the rope and studied it. What did this mean?

In the basement, Danny was still trying to catch up with the Zathura game before it reached the fire. As he ran beside the conveyor belt, he tripped, heard a wet squishing sound, and looked down. He had stepped in some sort of glow-in-the-dark space goop. Actually, it looked kind of like a pile of . . .

"Ew!" said Danny.

He kept running, following the game, until he bumped into something alive. It was covered with long hair.

He heard a bleat.

"It's just a goat," Danny said to himself, wishing he could believe it. "Just a goat . . ."

The "goat" turned and looked at him. Six eyes on stalks sprang out in his direction.

"Not a goat. Not a goat," mumbled Danny. He looked up, saw more creatures, and scrambled away, totally freaked. In his haste, he knocked loose the chain restraining the livestock. They were now free-range space goats, leaping into the basement and out of captivity.

There was no time to think about this, though, because the conveyor belt was still relentlessly moving, and the game had almost reached the fire. A Zorgon was at the end of the belt, shoveling junk into the blaze. This meant that Danny had no way of getting the game back without being seen.

But the space goats, returning the favor to Danny, saved the day. The shoveling Zorgon noticed that they were loose, turned to look, and gave chase. While the lizard was distracted, Danny raced over to the game, already inside the ship, and snatched it off the belt. Then he jumped down, ducked under the belt, scrambled over a junk pile, and ran like crazy.

Praying that the Zorgons would not notice him, he bolted across the basement and leaped into the dumbwaiter chute, which was still hanging by the rope. He clambered into the box and whispered into the chute: "Pull me up! Hey, you guys, pull me up!" Reaching out of the box, he tugged on the rope a few times to get their attention.

Upstairs on the landing, the Zorgon, which had been staring at the rope, jumped back in alarm as it bounced in front of him, pulled by Danny from below. The thing was alive!

The Zorgon barked at the rope, raised his sword, and cut right through it with a single slice.

Danny was still tugging on the rope. "Come on!" he whispered desperately. Suddenly it went slack and fell down the chute, dropping into a useless pile of hemp at his feet. The dumbwaiter dropped the last few inches to the bottom of the shaft with a thud.

"Oh, no," moaned Danny.

Near the blast furnace, the shoveling Zorgon had

returned to the end of the conveyor belt, still trying to figure out how the space goats had gotten loose. The Zorgon did a double take, looking at something on the floor.

Footprints! Footprints in glowing green space-goat poop.

Danny's tracks could clearly be seen running under the conveyor belt, over the junk pile, and into the basement.

The Zorgon barked at the top of its lungs and drew its sword.

Still in the dumbwaiter, Danny watched in alarm as the Zorgon appeared in the doorway of the ship, barking frantically at its companions. They all turned and spotted Danny.

Danny squirmed out of the dumbwaiter box and took off across the basement as fast as he could, toward the stairs. The Zorgons gave chase. But Danny was little, and little meant maneuverable. He ran and leaped through a stack of built-in shelves just as the Zorgons were catching up to him. He fell, but at least the Zorgons were at bay for the moment, unable to get through the shelves. Danny jumped back to his feet, ran for the basement door, and turned the doorknob.

Locked!

"OPEN THE DOOR! SOMEBODY OPEN THE DOOR! I'M COMING! OPEN THE DOOR!" he screamed.

A disgusting Zorgon tongue slithered between the shelves and flicked across the back of Danny's neck. "Ewwww!" he yelped.

*Crash!* Behind Danny, the Zorgons were chopping the daylights out of the bookshelves with their swords.

Danny was banging on the basement door as hard as he could, but it was no use—the Zorgons had him pinned now.

Suddenly, the doorknob turned and the door swung open. Walter grabbed Danny and hauled him out of the basement, slamming and bolting the door behind them.

"Walter!" said Danny. He hugged Walter as hard as he could, fighting back the tears of relief.

"Told you I wouldn't let anything happen to you!" said Walter.

The brothers were not out of the woods, not by a long shot. At the top of the stairs, in the kitchen, two more Zorgon lizards appeared. Walter and Danny screamed. They were doomed for sure—stuck on the stairs, killer lizards above and below, no way out of this one. The Zorgons above snarled, and the Zorgons below barked and spat.

But what was that sound? It was horrifying—the sound of utter chaos from behind the basement door. They could hear crashing and banging and the squeals of Zorgons. Both the Zorgons upstairs and the two boys below were stopped in their tracks by it.

There was a second of silence. Then the lower door exploded into toothpicks, revealing the repaired robot in all its glory, blowing steam from its nose. Its eyes were blazing red again. It was covered with green goo. "AUTO-REPAIR COMPLETE," said the robot.

Danny and Walter shouted in triumph, but not for long. The robot turned, its eyes now blazing at Walter. "ALIEN LIFE FORM," said the robot. "MUST

DESTROY." Their shouts of triumph changed instantly to screams of despair.

"He still wants to kill me!" yelled Walter.

"The card!" shouted Danny. "Use the CARD!"

Remembering, Walter fumbled in his pocket for the card the game had given him earlier.

The robot's red beams fell squarely on Walter's chest.

Walter pulled the card out, held it in front of him like a badge, and shouted, "REPROGRAM!"

The robot beeped. Then a series of rapid boops and hums emitted from its processor.

The upstairs Zorgons continued to watch curiously.

The robot lurched forward, stomping toward the boys, its heavy feet smashing through the basement stairs. In a second, it was looming over them. Its arms shot out . . . and gently pushed the boys aside.

Its red eye-beams shifted, then split in two and landed on the Zorgons at the top of the stairs. "ALIEN LIFE FORMS! MUST DESTROY!" it chanted. The robot's afterburners popped out of its back and it took off like a guided missile, flying straight up the stairs.

The Zorgons bolted, heading back toward the living room. The robot slammed into the wall where they had been standing.

Walter and Danny ran upstairs to watch as the two

Zorgons fleeing the robot raced back into the foyer, barking and snarling in fear.

The robot bounced off the back wall and turned in pursuit, breaking out its spinning, whining circular saw blades. Making a mad dash down the hall toward the front of the house, it just missed the Zorgons as they leaped up to the ceiling—giant lizard leaps that carried them all the way up through the hole in the roof and into their ship.

But the robot wasn't satisfied. As the Zorgon hatchway started to slide shut, the robot's afterburners kicked in again and it blasted off, straight up, just squeezing through the hatch before it closed.

Frantic screams could be heard coming from inside the ship as it took off with its new passenger. Green goop spattered up against one of the portholes. The ship careened away into deep space, twisting and turning as the robot wreaked its havoc inside.

"I guess that's what the reprogram card's for," said Walter.

"I like that card," said Danny.

"I think that's the last of them," said Walter.

But when Walter and Danny looked out the window, they saw a huge swarm of Zorgon ships converging on the house, firing as they approached. Walter and Danny stood watching through the hole in the roof.

"Where's the game?" Danny asked. If they were

going to leave these Zorgon ships behind, they were going to have to finish the game, and fast.

Unseen by the boys, one last Zorgon who had gotten left behind was sneaking down the stairs behind them.

"The astronaut guy has it," said Walter.

"Where's Lisa?" said Danny.

The Zorgon reached slowly out to grab them from behind. Its nauseating tongue snaked out toward them.

*WHAM.*

The piano came barreling down the stairs and slammed into the Zorgon with a discordant bang, knocking the lizard out through the wall.

The boys looked around to see what had happened.

Lisa was at the top of the stairs, having just launched the deadly instrument. She answered Danny's question with satisfaction. "Lisa's upstairs," she said.

She came downstairs, followed by the astronaut, who had the game, and the four of them made their way to the den, navigating the shattered floorboards as they walked. Only space and stars and swarming Zorgon ships were below them if they slipped.

*Bam!* Another fiery flash came from the hostile ships.

They fled into the den and locked the door

behind them. Here, they had a moment of peace from the chaos outside.

*Crack!* The house shuddered. A direct hit.

"What are you waiting for?" said the astronaut. "Spin!"

Danny slapped the game down in the middle of the floor, and they dived down to it. "My turn!" he said. He twisted the key and hit the spinner button, and the spinner came up nine.

Danny's piece moved ahead, the card came out, and the astronaut grabbed it for him. "I got it!" he said. "'Flunk space academy, go back a space,'" he read.

Everyone looked at Danny, expecting him to be mad, but he simply blinked. "I'm not even going to comment on that," he said.

*BOOM.* Another Zorgon hit.

"My turn," said Walter quickly. Crank! Smack! Spin!

Three.

Walter's rocket ship rattled ahead and the board spat out a card, which he snatched up and read. "'Hit time warp. Go back three spaces and repeat last turn.'"

His piece moved back three spaces, which landed him right back on the wishing star. His eyes lit up. "I get another wish!" he yelled.

Immediately, they all winced as a blinding light

shined through their windows. They turned and looked. A shooting star was approaching, just like the one that Walter had wished on before.

Walter looked at the astronaut. "Thanks for helping us out," he said.

The astronaut nodded and smiled. Walter closed his eyes and whispered his wish: *"I wish the astronaut had his brother back."*

The star passed the house with its hot sizzling sound, and the light turned a brilliant white. They all turned away and covered their eyes, temporarily blinded.

Finally, it passed. The light faded. They all turned back toward the windows as they were slowly able to see again.

But they could not believe what they were seeing.

Standing in front of the windows was another Danny. A little cleaner, but otherwise exactly identical.

The astronaut's jaw dropped, and so did everybody else's.

Danny Two looked around, just as confused as the others, trying to figure out where he was. "You wished for two of me?" he said.

Walter panicked. "No!" he cried. "I wished the astronaut got his brother back!"

The astronaut fell to his knees and held Danny Two by the shoulders. "Danny," he said, his voice full of emotion.

"Who are you?" said Danny Two.

The astronaut hugged Danny Two close to him, overwhelmed. "Your brother," he said. "Walter."

"What?" said Walter.

"What?" said Danny.

"No, you're not," said Danny Two.

"Yes," said the astronaut. "I'm older, but I'm him. I came back for you."

"What's going on?" said Walter.

Danny Two turned to hear young Walter's voice, then saw Danny gaping back at him. The room was tense as the rest of them watched the two Dannys.

Danny Two walked over to Danny. They both slowly held up their hands to each other, as if they were on opposite sides of a mirror. As soon as they touched, Danny Two got sucked into Danny. They melded.

Danny looked back to the others, wide-eyed. "That was awesome!" he said.

Walter was dumbfounded. The astronaut turned to look him in the eye, and he walked toward Walter, his younger self.

Walter looked confused and more than a little freaked out.

"Thank you," said the astronaut.

"I . . . I . . ." was all Walter was able to say.

"You did good. You did better than I did."

"Okay," said Walter.

"Now make sure he gets home safe," said the astronaut. He reached out and touched Walter.

Right before Walter's eyes, time reversed itself.

The astronaut got younger and younger until he was Walter's age once again. And then he was sucked into Walter, just as Danny Two had been sucked into Danny.

After a blur of protoplasm, the astronaut was gone, as if he had never existed.

There was a long silence. "He was . . . me?" Walter said finally.

"Yeah," said Danny.

Lisa shuddered. "Oh my God, and I wanted to—"

*BLAMMM!* The house shook as a missile hit the room.

*KABOOM!* The front door of the house exploded off its hinges, hit by a Zorgon blast.

They could still hear the explosions outside. All three of them hit the deck around the game board. "Hurry up!" said Walter.

Outside, the swarm of Zorgon ships was circling the house in big lazy arcs, like mosquitoes around a porch light. Ships' harpoons and cables were ripping off the house's walls. More and more and more specks, Zorgon ships, were visible on the distant horizon. This was not going to end well.

Walter, Danny, and Lisa were flat on their stomachs, covering their heads from the falling debris as the house was attacked.

"Ten!" Walter yelled. "You need a ten to win!"

Danny slammed the button and the big wheel spun.

One of the circling Zorgon ships directed a fire blast at the top of the house, which burst into flame. They were going to destroy the house right here, right now.

The wheel landed on . . . one. "One! God, I suck!" wailed Danny.

His rocket ship motored ahead one space toward the round black sphere of Zathura, which waited at the end of the trail.

A game card popped out. Walter read: "'Would you like to swing on a star? Move ahead nine spaces.' You did it! You won!"

Danny was ecstatic. "I did it. I got a ten!" he yelled, jumping up and down.

They all jumped up and down with him, and hugged and yelled. Meanwhile, Danny's rocket was rattling down its track on the board, closing in on the final space: the black planet Zathura.

But something was not right. The game started to shake, and then the sphere at the end of the game began to spin and open, like a flower blooming. In the middle was a black round thing.

"What is it?" said Walter.

"It doesn't look like a planet to me!" Danny said.

The windows went dark, and the house began to spin. Things began to slide around the room. They looked out the window.

There it was: Zathura. It was a gigantic, swirling

black mass, so huge that it occupied nearly their entire field of vision. Everyone grabbed something to hold on to as the strong pull of the mass sent everything flying.

Now they were moving fast, *really* fast, headed straight toward it.

"IT'S A BLACK HOLE!" yelled Danny. "ZATHURA IS A BLACK HOLE!"

It was a black hole, all right, and it was pulling them and everything else into it. As the house tumbled and spun toward the black void, they could see Zorgon ships ahead of them, attempting to escape as they were sucked in.

Then house itself began to come apart.

The entire back wall came off. Books, lamps, furniture, everything not nailed down sailed out the back of the house and disappeared into Zathura. Everybody screamed as the house kept rushing helplessly toward the black hole, twisting and bucking, until suddenly—

Danny was still screaming, but he was sitting on the living room floor now, and the living room was brightly lit, the same way it had been before the whole thing started. They had popped out of the black hole.

Sunlight streamed in. Trees stood outside the window, and Walter was sitting with his back to Danny, as he'd been at the beginning, slumped in the chair in front of the TV set, watching *SportsCenter.*

Danny stopped screaming and looked around, utterly disoriented. He looked down to find that his red rocket ship game piece was resting on the planet Earth again. Walter's blue ship was back in the box. The board was spread out in front of him, and Danny's hand was outstretched, ready to push the button for the first time.

He turned, his hand frozen in midair, and looked at Walter. "Walter?" he said.

Walter turned around slowly and stared at him. His eyes were as wide as saucers. "Don't. Push. That. Button," he said.

*Veeeeeeerrrrry* carefully, Danny stood up and backed away from the game.

Walter got up out of his chair. They stared at the board for a second, and then at each other.

"WE DID IT! WE DID IT!" they shouted together.

Danny hurled himself at Walter and tackled him, and they both fell backwards onto the carpet. Walter wrestled Danny off him and they rolled around on the floor, but it was playful this time: Walter was laughing—they were both laughing.

And then Dad came through the door.

"I distinctly remember asking you guys not to kill each other," he said.

"Dad!" yelled Danny joyously. They both hurled themselves at their father, and he went down to the carpet, and all three of them were on the floor, rolling around like crazy people. The boys talked a mile a minute, their words tumbling over each other.

Walter said, "Dad there was this game and it sent the house into outer space and everything got wrecked and we almost had to stay in it forever and I saw myself grown up and—"

Danny said, "It was so scary there were these lizard guys and we went through a black hole and I stole the game back from the Zorgons I wasn't scared and—"

"Wow, sounds like fun!" said Dad. "Hey, your mom's gonna be here any minute. Go grab all the books and games and whatever you wanna take to her house. It's almost three."

He got up from the floor and went upstairs, whistling.

The boys looked at each other, realizing there was

no point in telling Dad later. No one would ever believe this.

"But you and me know, right?" said Danny.

"You and me," said Walter, nodding.

Then Danny saw something on the floor and broke into a huge grin. It was his gerbil, playing around in his cage, safe and sound. Danny ran to him. "Richard!" he cried, kissing his furry old pal.

A car pulled up in front of the house and honked twice. Dad came downstairs and waved to the car from the open doorway. He turned and bent down to help Danny put on his backpack. "I'll miss you, kiddo," he said, "but I'll see you on Wednesday."

Danny tried to zip his jacket, but it wouldn't go up. Dad helped him. Then he brushed Danny's hair out of his eyes and kissed him. "I love you," he said.

Walter was hurrying to get ready, zipping his own coat, his backpack already on. Dad kissed him as well. "And I love you too," he said.

Walter and Danny headed out the door, walking down the lawn toward their mom.

As they took the short walk from one parent to the other, Walter looked at his brother. "So, what do you think happened to the astronaut guy?" he said.

"You were the astronaut guy."

"Oh. Right. In the future."

"In what would've been the future," Danny said, working it out in his head.

"Oh. Right."

At the last minute, Lisa came running out of the house, her jammed backpack over her shoulder. She looked a wreck. Her hair was all over the place, and there were dark circles under her eyes. She bent down between the boys as she passed them. "We never speak of this," she said. "Got it?"

"Sure," said Danny.

"Whatever," shrugged Walter.

She stomped toward the car, blew past her mother, got into the front seat, and slammed the door behind her.

As Walter stood on the lawn, watching her, a smile crossed his face. "You still think I have gorgeous eyes?" he called after her.

The sun was shining, and they hadn't been destroyed by the black hole or eaten by Zorgons. Walter was feeling great. He grabbed his brother by the backpack and dragged him around in happy circles with it. Dad was standing in the doorway, Mom was waiting in the car, and the two boys began walking down the sidewalk. It was a good day.

And then Walter's bike fell from the sky and landed on the front lawn.